400 Years Of Silence: The Journey from Prophecy to Messiah

J.J. Holt

Published by J.J. Holt, 2024.

400 YEARS OF SILENCE: THE JOURNEY FROM PROPHECY TO MESSIAH

First edition. September 13, 2024.

ISBN: 979-8227299352

Written by J.J. Holt.

Table of Contents

To my beloved wife Louisa and our wonderful children, Aubire, Conry, Riker, and Avery. Your love, strength, and endless support make every step of this journey possible. This story is for you, now and always.

Prologue

Jerusalem, 167 BCE

Darkness settled over Jerusalem like a suffocating shroud. Smoke from burning scrolls twisted into the night sky, carrying with it the bitter scent of desecration. The cries of those who defied the king echoed through the streets, each voice silenced too soon by the edge of a sword.

Elijah stood motionless in the shadows, his back pressed against the cold stone wall of the alley. His heart thundered in his chest, pounding louder than the chaos that had engulfed his city. A bead of sweat traced a line down his face, mixing with the dust and ash that clung to his skin. He had known fear before—had felt it every time his father whispered of Antiochus' growing rage—but this... this was something else. This was terror.

Before him, in the square where the temple once stood, a bonfire raged, fed by the torn and shredded remnants of the Torah. Each sacred word consumed by the flames felt like a dagger in Elijah's heart, and with it came a deeper wound, one that no blade could inflict. They were destroying the very soul of his people.

"Please... have mercy," a voice called out, and Elijah's breath caught in his throat.

His father.

Elijah's eyes darted to the center of the square, where his father, kneeling in the dirt, hands bound, faced the iron-clad soldiers of the Seleucid king. Behind him, his mother and younger sister knelt as well, their faces pale with fear but resolute, refusing to bow to the altar of Zeus erected in the heart of the holy city.

"I will not bend," his father's voice cracked, but his words carried across the square. "We are servants of the One True God, and we will not bow to false idols."

The captain sneered, his sword glinting in the firelight. "Your God is nothing but smoke and dust. Antiochus rules here now. You will submit, or you will die."

Elijah gripped the stone wall tighter, his fingers digging into the cracks, as if he could hold himself together by sheer force of will. He wanted to cry out, to run to his family, to beg them to flee. But his feet were frozen, and his voice locked behind clenched teeth. He could only watch.

His mother spoke then, her voice a soft murmur carried on the wind. "We are not afraid. The Lord is our shepherd."

The captain gave a slow, deliberate nod before raising his sword high. "Then let Him save you."

The blade came down in a blur of steel. Blood sprayed across the stone courtyard. His father crumpled. Elijah felt the ground beneath him tilt, but still, he could not move.

His mother was next. She did not scream. Her lips moved in silent prayer, her eyes fixed on the heavens above as the sword found her neck. Then his sister... her young face frozen in terror, but brave, so brave. It was over in seconds, and yet those seconds would stretch out in Elijah's mind for eternity.

Elijah's knees buckled, but he did not fall. Not yet. The burning scrolls crackled louder now, as if mocking him, as if the very words of God were being devoured by the darkness closing in. His family's blood soaked the ground, mingling with the ash and embers of the scriptures.

He wanted to cry. He wanted to scream. But something else surged inside him, something hotter than the flames in the square—rage, yes, but more than that. A fierce resolve.

He stepped back into the shadows, retreating from the carnage, his heart now set on a single, unshakable vow.

He would not let them destroy all that was sacred.

The Torah was more than ink on parchment. It was life. It was the voice of God, and if that voice was silenced, then all of Israel would be lost.

The words of the prophets swirled in his mind, promises of a Messiah, of redemption to come. But that day seemed distant now, shrouded in the smoke of destruction. For now, the only thing that mattered was keeping the Word alive.

Elijah swore silently as he slipped away into the night. He would not let their sacrifices be in vain. He would preserve the holy scriptures, even if it cost him his life. He did not know how or when, but a plan was unfolding—he could feel it, like a tremor beneath his feet, a divine calling he could not yet comprehend.

And in that moment, as the fires of Jerusalem burned behind him, Elijah became a guardian of the unseen. The words of God would live, even in darkness.

Act I: The Descent into Darkness

Chapter 1: A Silent Rebellion

The room was suffocating in its silence, save for the slow scratching of a quill across parchment. Elijah's hand trembled as he wrote, his focus sharpening the strokes, perfecting each letter with a precision that felt ritualistic. Around him, the dim light of oil lamps flickered against the rough-hewn walls, casting long shadows on the scrolls piled high. In those shadows, Elijah sought refuge, but there was no comfort to be found there. Not anymore.

His hands froze mid-stroke as the memory of his family—his father, mother, and sister—flashed before his eyes. He could still hear his father's voice, defiant even in the face of death. He could still see the blood, fresh in his mind like it had happened only moments ago. They had died for this, for the words now etched beneath his fingers, and their sacrifice weighed heavy on his soul. Each letter, each line of sacred text was a tether to a world that no longer existed for him—a world where his family was alive, and where the temple still stood as the heart of their faith.

"Elijah." The voice broke the silence, soft but firm.

He flinched, realizing his hand had frozen over the parchment for too long. His mentor, Ezra, sat across from him, watching with eyes that carried both sorrow and wisdom far beyond the confines of the small room. Elijah had always admired Ezra's unwavering faith. Even now, in the face of desecration and destruction, Ezra's belief in the divine plan was steadfast.

"Elijah," Ezra repeated, his voice gentle yet commanding. "You've been staring at that page for some time. There's no need to rush the work."

Elijah swallowed hard, placing the quill down carefully beside the scroll. "I'm not rushing," he murmured, his voice hoarse. "I... I just can't stop thinking about them. About what happened."

Ezra nodded slowly. "Your family's sacrifice was not in vain. You must know this."

Elijah's jaw tightened, his eyes falling to the scroll before him. The holy words blurred in his vision, overtaken by the image of his father's final moments, his mother's whispered prayer, and the terror etched into his sister's young face.

"They're all dead," Elijah whispered, his voice breaking. "How can that not be in vain? Everything's been taken from us, Ezra. The temple is in ruins, our people are hunted. Even the scrolls—they burn them as if they're nothing more than firewood."

Ezra leaned forward, his gaze sharp yet compassionate. "These words, Elijah—these scrolls—they are not just ink and parchment. They are life. They are the voice of God." He reached out, placing a firm hand on Elijah's shoulder. "Antiochus and his armies think they can destroy the sacred, but they do not understand. The Word of God is eternal. It cannot be destroyed by flame or sword."

Elijah blinked, feeling the weight of Ezra's words settle into him, but the grief—no, the anger—burned too hot beneath his skin. He couldn't see past the rage, the helplessness that had consumed him since that terrible night. "And yet, my father's blood stains the stones of the square. My mother... my sister..." His throat tightened, choking the words. "Where was God when they needed Him?"

Ezra sighed, the kind of sigh that carried the burden of countless years and untold grief. "He was with them, Elijah. Even in their suffering. You must believe this."

Elijah clenched his fists, the leather of his tunic creaking under the pressure. He wanted to believe. He wanted to hold on to the faith that had sustained him for so long, the faith that had shaped his family's every action. But the pain of loss was a wound too deep, too raw to heal with words alone.

He stood abruptly, the stool scraping the floor behind him. "What am I supposed to do with that?" he asked, his voice rising. "Believe in a God who lets us suffer? A God who allows our people to be slaughtered like animals in the street?" He shook his head, taking a step back from the table, from Ezra. "I don't know if I can do this."

Ezra remained seated, his calm a stark contrast to Elijah's rising fury. "You feel betrayed by God," he said softly, as if speaking the words for Elijah who could not. "But you must understand, this suffering—it was foretold. The prophets warned us that darkness would come before the light."

Elijah turned away, his heart hammering in his chest. His eyes fell on the pile of scrolls on the floor, remnants of what had been saved from the temple before its desecration. The priests and scribes had risked their lives to rescue what they could, hiding the sacred texts in caves, in cellars, anywhere the enemy wouldn't look. But so many had been lost.

"Do you remember the words of Daniel?" Ezra asked, his voice still soft, but carrying the weight of something far more than a mere question. "Do you remember what was written about the 'abomination of desolation'?"

Elijah stilled, his mind dredging up the words he had been taught since he was a child. He could recite them from memory, every line, every prophecy that Daniel had spoken about the time of destruction that would befall Jerusalem. But until now, those prophecies had been distant—stories of a future he never believed he would live to see.

Ezra rose to his feet, slowly approaching him. "This is that time, Elijah. Antiochus has set up his idols in our holy places. He has brought desolation to the temple, just as Daniel foresaw." He paused, letting the gravity of the words sink in. "But it is not the end."

Elijah turned to face him, confusion and bitterness warring in his expression. "How can you say that? How can you believe this is anything but the end? They've destroyed everything."

Ezra shook his head. "Not everything. The Word of God still remains, and we are its keepers now. We are the ones who must preserve it, protect it, until the time of redemption comes."

"Redemption?" Elijah's voice was thick with disbelief. "What redemption? We are slaves, Ezra. We are dying."

Ezra's eyes gleamed, and for the first time since the temple's destruction, Elijah saw something in them—a fire, a hope that had not yet been extinguished. "You cannot see it now, but the prophecies speak of more than destruction. They speak of deliverance. A Messiah will come, Elijah. And when He does, all of this suffering will be washed away."

Elijah's heart thudded against his ribs. A Messiah. He had heard the prophecies, of course—every child of Israel had—but they had always seemed so far away, part of a distant future that felt disconnected from the harsh realities of their present lives. Now, though, standing in the dim light of the room with Ezra's words hanging heavy in the air, something began to stir within him.

"What if..." Ezra's voice dropped, almost to a whisper. "What if we are not just victims of this darkness, but part of the plan to bring about the light? What if we are the ones who must keep the truth alive, until the time is right?"

Elijah's mind raced, his thoughts colliding with each other in a chaotic swirl of disbelief, hope, and fear. It was too much, too soon. The idea that he could be part of something so much larger than himself, that the suffering of his family could be part of a divine plan—it felt impossible to grasp.

And yet, deep down, there was a flicker of something—a tiny spark, buried beneath layers of anger and grief.

Ezra stepped closer, his voice gentle but insistent. "You feel lost now, Elijah. I understand. But there is more at work here than we can see. The scrolls we protect, the Word we preserve—it is all part of the greater story. The story of redemption."

Elijah swallowed, his throat dry. The weight of Ezra's words pressed down on him like a mantle, heavy and daunting, but also... purposeful. For the first time since his family's death, he felt something beyond rage—something that felt like direction.

He exhaled slowly, his shoulders sagging under the invisible burden. "What do we do?" he asked, his voice barely audible.

Ezra smiled softly, his eyes full of compassion. "We continue the work. We protect the Word. And we wait for the day when the Messiah comes to fulfill the prophecies."

Elijah nodded slowly, though he still wasn't sure he fully understood. But he knew one thing with absolute certainty: he couldn't walk away. Not now. Not after everything that had happened. His family's sacrifice, the blood that had stained the stones of the square—it couldn't be for nothing. He had to believe there was a reason, even if he couldn't see it yet.

Taking a deep breath, Elijah stepped back toward the table, his hand reaching once more for the quill. The scroll lay open before him, waiting. The sacred words had endured centuries, had survived fire and bloodshed, and they would continue to survive. As long as he could draw breath, he would see to that.

Ezra returned to his seat across the table, watching him with quiet approval. "One day, Elijah," he said softly, "you will see. All of this—our work, our suffering—it is part of the prophecy. It is part of God's plan."

Elijah dipped the quill into the ink, his hand steadying. The letters began to form once more, each stroke purposeful, deliberate.

He didn't fully understand it yet, but he was beginning to feel it—the pull of something greater, something far beyond the destruction and chaos that had engulfed his world.

The rebellion had begun, not with swords or fire, but with the silent preservation of words. And Elijah would be its keeper.

Chapter 2: Under Antiochus' Shadow

The night air in Jerusalem had become as thick and oppressive as the rule of Antiochus himself. Every street, every alley, felt like it was being watched. Soldiers, loyal to the king who had proclaimed himself a god, prowled the city like wolves, hungry for those who dared to defy the king's decrees. It was in this suffocating atmosphere that Ezra, Elijah, and the others worked tirelessly, desperate to preserve what was left of their faith, of their people.

Elijah moved quickly through the narrow streets, his heart racing, though his face remained calm, focused. The scroll beneath his arm—wrapped in old, tattered cloth—felt like it was burning a hole into his skin. He glanced around, pulling his cloak tighter around him, concealing his precious cargo. It wasn't just the Torah he was protecting. It was everything. Every word, every promise, every thread of hope.

In the distance, the temple stood like a ghost, its sanctity torn away, replaced by the grotesque image of Zeus towering over the ruins. His stomach twisted at the sight, but he forced himself to keep moving, ducking into the shadows as a pair of soldiers passed by, their armor gleaming even in the dim light of the moon.

The meeting place was a small house, tucked behind a row of crumbling stone walls, hidden from the main road. He knocked twice on the door, then paused. A moment later, it opened just enough for a woman's face to appear.

"Elijah," she whispered, stepping back to allow him inside. Miriam's voice, even when soft, held a strength that few others possessed.

He stepped in quickly, careful not to let the door creak as it closed. "Is Ezra here?"

Miriam nodded, her eyes sharp with the same tension that had become a constant companion to them all. She moved back to the corner of the room where Ezra sat, his brow furrowed in deep thought. A small group of scribes huddled nearby, their faces pale in the flickering candlelight.

"We don't have much time," Miriam said as Elijah joined them. She crossed her arms, the weight of responsibility heavy on her shoulders. "The soldiers are everywhere tonight. They're rounding up more families."

Elijah clenched his jaw. "How many this time?"

Miriam shook her head. "Too many. They aren't even pretending to offer a choice anymore. Submit or die."

Ezra's eyes opened slowly, his gaze steady despite the news. He was always calm, always composed, as if he could see something none of them could. Something beyond the violence and chaos. "It is as the prophecies foretold," he said quietly. "But we must not be distracted by fear. What we do here is more important than ever."

Elijah glanced down at the scroll he held, placing it carefully on the table before them. "We've secured another. But the soldiers are growing more violent. It won't be long before they turn their eyes on us."

"We need to move them," Miriam said, stepping forward. "We've hidden as many scrolls as we can, but the city is no longer safe. Not for us, and not for these."

Ezra nodded slowly, his expression grave. "You're right. Jerusalem is falling under a darkness deeper than any of us could have imagined. It is time."

"Time for what?" Elijah asked, though a part of him already knew the answer. He'd felt it for weeks, a sense of inevitability hanging over them like a storm cloud.

"To leave," Ezra replied, his voice firm. "We must take the scrolls and go where Antiochus' soldiers cannot find us. Qumran."

The word hung in the air between them, a name spoken like a secret, like a prayer.

Miriam's brow furrowed. "The desert?"

Ezra's gaze shifted to her, understanding the weight of her question. "Yes. The desert. It is where we will be safest. The community there is dedicated to the preservation of our sacred texts. They will welcome us, and together, we will protect the Word."

Elijah felt a strange mixture of relief and dread settle in his chest. Relief, because staying in Jerusalem was a death sentence. But dread, because the desert was unforgiving. And leaving Jerusalem felt like abandoning the fight.

"How will we get the scrolls there?" Elijah asked, his mind already racing with the logistics. "We can't carry them all ourselves. Not without being caught."

Ezra leaned back, his eyes narrowing slightly as though deep in thought. "We'll need help. Trusted help."

Miriam shifted, her face darkening for a moment. "Jonas," she said quietly.

Elijah's heart skipped a beat at the name. Jonas. The mere mention of him filled the room with unspoken tension.

"Jonas?" Ezra echoed, as if weighing the possibility.

"He's still serving in the army," Miriam continued, her voice steady but laced with something Elijah couldn't quite identify. "But he's one of us. He's been helping families escape, guiding them through the checkpoints. We can trust him."

Elijah wasn't so sure. "He's a soldier in Antiochus' army," he said, his voice harder than he intended. "How can we trust him?"

Miriam's gaze met his, sharp and unwavering. "Because he's risking his life every day for us. His loyalty isn't to Antiochus. It's to his people."

Elijah wanted to believe her. He really did. But there was something about Jonas—something Elijah couldn't put his finger on. The man was torn, that much was clear. But torn men made dangerous decisions.

"We'll need him," Ezra said finally, cutting through the tension. "If we're going to escape with the scrolls, we need someone who knows the army's movements. Someone who can get us through the city unnoticed."

Elijah wanted to argue, wanted to push back, but Ezra's decision was final. He nodded, though the unease settled deep in his bones.

Later that night, Miriam and Elijah sat by a small fire, tucked in the corner of the old house, its warmth providing little comfort in the face of the cold reality around them.

"You don't trust him," Miriam said, her voice quiet, but direct. She didn't look at him, her eyes instead focused on the flames dancing in the hearth.

Elijah glanced at her, surprised by how well she could read him. "Do you?"

Miriam's lips pressed into a thin line. "Jonas is complicated. But he's not the enemy. He's lost... in many ways. But he's trying."

"Trying to help us, or trying to help himself?" Elijah asked, his tone sharper than he intended.

Miriam turned to him then, her gaze hard. "You think you're the only one who's lost something to Antiochus? My brother was part of the revolt last year. He fought with everything he had. And when the soldiers came to our house, they didn't ask questions. They just killed him."

Elijah blinked, his anger melting away into something closer to shame. He hadn't known about her brother. He'd only known Miriam as the fierce, determined woman who had thrown herself into helping their people, who had never once shown a crack in her resolve.

"I'm sorry," Elijah whispered.

Miriam shrugged, her eyes turning back to the fire. "It's not about being sorry. It's about fighting for something bigger than yourself. My brother died for the same reason your family did. For our faith. For the Word." She paused, her expression hardening. "Jonas didn't pull the trigger, but he's been part of that machine. He knows it. And he's trying to make up for it."

Elijah stared at her, seeing her in a new light. She was more than just a fellow scribe, more than just a helper in their mission. She was a warrior in her own right, forged in fire and loss, just as he had been.

"You believe in him," Elijah said softly.

Miriam nodded, though her eyes still held a shadow of doubt. "I do. But it's not easy. Jonas is still struggling with his own guilt. His own demons. But I think… I think he's with us."

Elijah sighed, running a hand through his hair. "I hope you're right."

The next evening, Jonas arrived, slipping through the back entrance like a ghost. His face was hard, lined with worry, but his eyes darted around the room, ever-watchful, ever-nervous.

"Elijah," he said, his voice low, barely a whisper.

Elijah gave him a curt nod, though the tension between them was palpable. Miriam stood nearby, her arms crossed as she watched the exchange.

"Ezra says you've agreed to help us," Elijah said, his words clipped.

Jonas' jaw tightened, his gaze flicking to the ground for a moment before returning to Elijah's. "I'll do what I can."

"And how far does that go?" Elijah pressed, his suspicion slipping through.

Jonas straightened, his face hardening. "I've been risking my life every day to help families escape this city. What more do you want from me?"

Elijah's eyes narrowed. "I want to know where your loyalty lies, Jonas. Are you one of us, or are you still serving Antiochus?"

A flash of anger crossed Jonas' face, and for a moment, Elijah thought he might storm out, that he'd pushed too far. But then Jonas spoke, his voice rough and low, almost broken. "I'm not serving Antiochus. I never was."

Miriam stepped forward, her voice softer. "We need you, Jonas. We can't get the scrolls out of Jerusalem without your help."

Jonas' eyes flicked to her, something softer in his expression. "I know. I'll do it. But it's dangerous. The soldiers are tightening their grip. They're searching every cart, every alley. If we're caught..." He trailed off, the meaning clear.

Ezra, who had been watching silently from the corner, stepped forward. "We all know the risk. But the Word is worth it. We must believe that."

Jonas nodded slowly, though the weight of their task clearly bore down on him. He turned to Elijah, his face set in grim determination. "I'll get you through the gates. But after that, you're on your own."

Elijah stared at him for a moment longer, then nodded. It wasn't trust, not fully, but it was something. And for now, it would have to be enough.

The days that followed were filled with tension, every movement calculated, every step shadowed by the threat of discovery. The soldiers were everywhere—at every gate, at every turn, their presence an oppressive reminder of the danger they faced.

Miriam worked tirelessly alongside Elijah, carefully wrapping the scrolls in cloth, concealing them in the bottom of carts filled with goods bound for the desert. The plan was simple, but fraught with peril. They would disguise themselves as traders, leaving the city under the cover of darkness, with Jonas guiding them through the checkpoints.

Elijah's heart pounded in his chest as the night of their escape drew near. The weight of the scrolls—both literal and symbolic—pressed down on him, the enormity of their task nearly overwhelming. If they were caught, if even one scroll was discovered, it would mean death for them all.

As they gathered in the small, hidden room one last time before the journey, Ezra spoke softly, his voice calm despite the gravity of the situation. "Remember, this is not just about us. What we carry is the future. The Word must survive, no matter the cost."

Elijah nodded, his hands trembling slightly as he gripped the cloth-wrapped scroll in his lap. Across from him, Miriam's face was set in grim determination, though her eyes betrayed the fear she kept hidden beneath the surface.

Jonas stood near the door, his gaze flicking between the window and the group, ever-watchful, ever-nervous. Elijah could see the tension in his shoulders, the guilt in his eyes. He was torn, that much was clear. Torn between his duty to the army and his loyalty to his people. Torn between fear and faith.

"Elijah," Ezra said, pulling his attention back to the present. "Are you ready?"

Elijah swallowed hard, his throat dry, but he nodded. "I'm ready."

Ezra gave him a small, sad smile, as if he could see the weight of the world on Elijah's shoulders. "Then let's go. God be with us all."

They moved like shadows through the streets, the carts creaking softly as they rolled toward the city gates. The silence was deafening, broken only by the occasional bark of a dog or the distant sound of soldiers patrolling the walls.

Elijah's heart pounded in his chest as they approached the gate, his hands gripping the reins of the donkey pulling the cart. Miriam walked beside him, her face pale in the dim moonlight, but her expression set with determination.

Jonas was already ahead, speaking quietly with the soldiers at the gate, his face a mask of calm. Elijah watched as the soldiers laughed at something Jonas said, their attention momentarily diverted.

"Now," Jonas whispered as he returned, his voice barely audible. "Move."

Elijah swallowed hard and urged the cart forward, his breath catching as they passed through the gate, the soldiers barely glancing at them.

Once they were through, Jonas turned to them, his expression grim. "You're free of the city now. But the desert... the desert is another challenge altogether."

Elijah nodded, glancing back at the gates of Jerusalem as they disappeared into the darkness. They had escaped the city, but the real journey had just begun.

Chapter 3: Fleeing to Qumran

The desert stretched before them like an endless sea of sand and rock, its unforgiving landscape illuminated by the faint glow of the moon. The wind howled, whipping the sand into their faces, stinging their skin, and yet, the silence between them was more deafening than the desert's roar.

Elijah walked with his head bowed, the weight of the scrolls strapped to his back pressing down on his shoulders like a burden far heavier than their physical form. Every step felt like an eternity, each grain of sand beneath his sandals dragging him closer to the edge of his resolve. His throat was parched, and his lips cracked from the dry air, but it wasn't just the desert that wore him down—it was the doubt gnawing at his mind.

Was this really part of God's plan? Had their people suffered so greatly only to flee into the wilderness, with no clear end in sight? He had grown up believing in the stories of the Exodus, in the idea that God led His people through the desert to a promised land. But now, with every step into the barren wasteland, he wondered if they were being led to nothing more than oblivion.

"Elijah," Miriam's voice called from behind him, breaking the silence.

He stopped, turning to see her approaching, her face hardened against the wind. She walked with a sense of purpose, her steps sure, even as exhaustion weighed on her just as it did the rest of them. She had proven herself essential to their journey, her practical skills keeping them alive when the desert sought to claim them. She carried no scrolls, only a single dagger at her side, her only burden the responsibility to protect those who carried the Word.

"You need to rest," she said, her voice firm but not unkind.

Elijah shook his head, glancing back at the small group of scribes who trailed behind them, their faces gaunt with fatigue. "We can't afford to stop. The soldiers—"

"The soldiers are at least a day behind us," Miriam interrupted, stepping closer. "We've been walking for hours, Elijah. We need to rest."

Elijah's eyes flickered with uncertainty, but as he looked into Miriam's gaze, he saw no room for argument. She was right. His body screamed for rest, his legs trembling with every step. He glanced at Jonas, who walked at the rear of the group, his eyes ever-watchful for any sign of pursuit. The former soldier said nothing, but his silence was louder than any word of protest. He too knew they were pushing too hard.

Elijah sighed, nodding slowly. "All right. We'll rest here."

Miriam gave a short nod, already moving to help the others find a place to sit amidst the rocky terrain. Elijah watched her for a moment, admiring her strength, her resolve. She moved with such purpose, such certainty, as if she alone could carry them all through the wilderness by sheer will.

As the group settled down, Elijah found a flat rock to rest on, his back aching as he removed the scrolls from his shoulders. The weight lifted, but the pressure in his chest remained. He glanced at the others—Ezra, with his calm, unwavering faith; Jonas, silent and brooding; the other scribes, weary but determined. They were all looking to him, to Ezra, for guidance. For hope.

But what hope could he offer them, when he wasn't even sure they were on the right path?

The desert was vast and cruel. They had been walking for days, and the only signs of life they had encountered were fleeting—a lone bird in the sky, a few scattered shrubs. The land was as barren as his faith had begun to feel.

"Elijah."

He looked up to see Miriam standing before him, her expression softening as she sat beside him. For a moment, neither of them spoke, the only sound between them the howling wind.

"You've been quiet," she said after a while, her eyes searching his face. "More than usual."

Elijah let out a bitter laugh, shaking his head. "What is there to say?"

Miriam raised an eyebrow. "You've never been at a loss for words before."

He sighed, rubbing a hand over his face, feeling the grit of sand against his skin. "I don't know, Miriam. I just... I don't know if we're doing the right thing."

Her gaze narrowed. "You think preserving the Word is the wrong thing?"

"No, of course not," Elijah said quickly, his voice tinged with frustration. "It's just... what if this isn't part of God's plan? What if we're just running into the wilderness with no purpose? What if—what if God isn't with us at all?"

Miriam was silent for a long moment, her eyes fixed on him. "You've lost your faith," she said quietly.

Elijah's throat tightened, his heart pounding in his chest. He wanted to deny it, to say that wasn't true, but the words caught in his throat. Had he lost his faith? He had been raised to believe in the God of Israel, the God of Abraham, Isaac, and Jacob. But now, after everything that had happened, after the desecration of the temple, after the slaughter of his family... where was God?

"I don't know," he whispered, his voice breaking. "I don't know anymore."

Miriam studied him, her gaze intense but not unkind. "You're not the only one who's questioned, Elijah. Do you think I haven't wondered the same thing? Do you think I haven't been angry? My brother was killed, just like your family. I've had every reason to turn away from God, to believe that He's abandoned us."

Elijah looked at her, surprised by the raw emotion in her voice. He had known Miriam was strong, but he hadn't realized the depth of her own grief, her own struggles.

"But I haven't," Miriam continued, her voice firm. "Because I refuse to believe that everything we've been through—everything we've lost—is for nothing. We are still here, Elijah. We are still alive. And as long as we carry the Word, as long as we protect the truth, then there is hope."

Elijah stared at her, his heart heavy with the weight of her words. He wanted to believe her, to hold on to the hope she spoke of. But the desert stretched out before them, vast and unyielding, and the soldiers were never far behind.

"Do you really believe that?" he asked softly. "That there's hope?"

Miriam met his gaze, her eyes filled with a quiet strength. "I do. And you should too."

Elijah exhaled slowly, feeling the tension in his chest ease, if only a little. He still wasn't sure. He still had doubts. But there was something about Miriam's conviction, her unwavering belief, that made him want to believe too.

"We should get some rest," Miriam said, rising to her feet. "We still have a long way to go."

Elijah nodded, watching as she walked away to check on the others. He sat in silence for a while longer, his mind a whirlwind of thoughts and doubts. But as the wind howled around him, carrying the faintest scent of distant rain, he felt a flicker of something deep within him. Something small, but undeniable.

Hope.

The next morning, they set off again, the rising sun casting long shadows across the desert floor. The heat bore down on them, relentless and unforgiving. The scrolls strapped to their backs felt heavier with each passing hour, the weight of their mission pressing down on their already weary bodies.

Jonas walked at the rear, his eyes scanning the horizon, ever-vigilant for signs of pursuit. He had grown more withdrawn as the journey progressed, speaking little, his face dark with unspoken thoughts. Elijah could sense the turmoil within him, the conflict that gnawed at his soul. Jonas had always been an enigma, a man torn between two worlds—his duty as a soldier, and his loyalty to his people.

"Elijah," Jonas called out quietly, falling into step beside him. His voice was rough, like gravel, a tone that hinted at the battles he fought within himself.

Elijah glanced at him, surprised by the sudden approach. They hadn't spoken much since leaving Jerusalem, and Elijah wasn't sure what to make of the man. He was a soldier, yes, but there was something else beneath the surface. Something hidden.

"What is it?" Elijah asked, his tone cautious.

Jonas hesitated for a moment, his gaze fixed on the horizon. "The soldiers... they're closer than we thought."

Elijah's heart skipped a beat. "How do you know?"

Jonas' jaw tightened. "I've been sabotaging their efforts. Slowing them down. But it won't be enough. They'll catch up to us eventually."

Elijah felt a chill run down his spine. The desert was dangerous enough without the threat of soldiers at their backs. If they were caught, it would mean certain death for them all—and the scrolls.

"Why are you telling me this?" Elijah asked, his voice low.

Jonas' gaze flicked to Miriam, who walked ahead of them, her shoulders squared against the heat of the sun. "Because you need to know what's coming. We can't outrun them forever."

Elijah followed his gaze, his chest tightening with a mixture of fear and frustration. He had known the risks, of course. They all had. But hearing it from

Jonas, hearing the certainty in his voice—it made the danger feel all the more real.

"What do you suggest we do?" Elijah asked, his voice laced with tension.

Jonas was silent for a moment, his brow furrowed in thought. "We can't fight them. Not out here. We're outnumbered, and we're carrying too much. But there's a ravine up ahead, not far from here. We could hide there. It might buy us some time."

Elijah nodded slowly, considering the plan. It wasn't much, but it was something. And right now, they needed every advantage they could get.

"We'll tell the others," Elijah said, his resolve hardening. "We'll make it to Qumran. We have to."

As they approached the ravine, the sun had begun to dip low on the horizon, casting long shadows across the rocky landscape. The group moved quickly, their bodies weary from days of travel, but their spirits bolstered by the hope that the ravine would provide them the cover they desperately needed.

The narrow path leading down into the ravine was treacherous, the rocks loose and jagged beneath their feet. Elijah led the way, his breath coming in shallow gasps as he navigated the steep incline. Behind him, Miriam followed, her steps sure, even as the others stumbled and struggled to keep up.

"Careful," she called out, reaching out to steady one of the scribes as he nearly lost his footing. "We're almost there."

Elijah glanced back at her, admiration flickering in his chest. She had become the protector of their group, her practical skills and unwavering determination keeping them alive when the desert sought to claim them. She had taken on a role far beyond that of a simple helper—she was their guide, their strength.

But even Miriam couldn't shield them from the dangers that lay ahead.

As they reached the bottom of the ravine, the group huddled together, their breath coming in ragged gasps. The walls of the ravine rose high around them, casting deep shadows that offered some relief from the sun's relentless heat. It was a temporary reprieve, but it wouldn't last long.

Jonas stood at the edge of the ravine, his eyes scanning the horizon once again. His face was a mask of concentration, but Elijah could see the tension in his posture, the conflict that simmered just beneath the surface.

"They're getting closer," Jonas muttered, his voice low. "We don't have much time."

Elijah's heart pounded in his chest as he looked at the others—Ezra, the scribes, Miriam. They were exhausted, their bodies worn down from the journey, but their resolve remained strong.

"What do we do now?" Elijah asked, his voice barely above a whisper.

Jonas was silent for a long moment, his eyes flicking to Miriam before returning to Elijah. "We keep moving. But if they find us... we fight."

As night fell, the desert's heat gave way to a bone-chilling cold that cut through their cloaks and skin. The stars above seemed cruelly distant, cold fires that mocked their struggle. They huddled together in the ravine, sharing what little warmth they could, but no one spoke. The weight of the journey and the impending threat hung over them like a shroud.

Elijah sat apart from the others, his back resting against the rocky wall of the ravine. He stared up at the stars, his thoughts churning like the sand in the wind. He had no answers, only questions—questions that gnawed at his soul, questions he was too afraid to voice.

Was this truly God's will? Was their mission part of some greater plan, or were they simply running from death, dragging the sacred scrolls into oblivion with them?

His mind returned to the prophecies, to the words of Daniel that Ezra had spoken of before they left Jerusalem. Daniel 8:9-14 spoke of the desecration of the temple, the destruction of everything they held sacred. But it also spoke of restoration, of a future where the temple would be cleansed, and their people redeemed.

Elijah closed his eyes, letting the words wash over him like a prayer. He wasn't sure if he believed them anymore, but he needed to. For the sake of the others, for the sake of the scrolls they carried—he had to believe.

Beside him, Miriam sat quietly, her presence a steady, grounding force amidst the chaos of his thoughts. She didn't speak, but somehow, her silence said more than words ever could.

"Do you think we'll make it?" Elijah asked softly, his voice barely audible over the sound of the wind.

Miriam turned to him, her eyes reflecting the faint light of the stars. "We have to."

Elijah nodded slowly, feeling the weight of her words settle into his bones. She was right. They had to make it. For the sake of the Word. For the sake of everything.

"We'll make it," he whispered, more to himself than to her. "We will."

And for the first time in days, Elijah felt a flicker of hope stir within him—small, fragile, but real.

As the darkness thickened around them, the ravine offered a false sense of security. The wind had died down, leaving only the eerie stillness of the desert night. The group huddled together, their exhaustion palpable.

Elijah sat with his back against the cold stone, his body aching from the journey. He had hoped the ravine would provide them with a few hours of safety, enough time to regain some strength before the final push toward Qumran. But even as he closed his eyes, trying to find some measure of peace, something gnawed at him.

Jonas.

Elijah's mind drifted back to the moments they had shared on the journey. Jonas had been quiet—too quiet. Even though he had warned them of the soldiers' approach, there was something about his demeanor, a tension in his voice that Elijah couldn't shake. Was it fear? Guilt? Or something more dangerous?

Miriam sat across from him, tending to a small fire. She glanced up, her eyes catching his. She had defended Jonas from the beginning, insisting that he was one of them. Elijah wanted to believe her, but a deep-rooted suspicion had taken hold of him, and he couldn't let it go.

"Elijah," Miriam whispered, drawing his attention. "You're not resting."

He shook his head. "I don't trust him."

Miriam frowned, her eyes flicking toward Jonas, who stood at the edge of the ravine, his back to them, keeping watch. "He's saved us more than once on this journey."

"And yet... something doesn't feel right."

Miriam sighed, her face softening. "I know you've been struggling, Elijah. With everything that's happened—your family, the temple. But Jonas is trying. He's one of us."

Before Elijah could respond, Jonas turned suddenly, his face pale in the firelight. "We need to move," he said, his voice low but urgent.

Elijah's heart skipped a beat. "What do you mean? You said we'd be safe here."

Jonas' gaze flickered, and for the briefest moment, Elijah saw it—fear. Guilt.

"I was wrong," Jonas said, his hand gripping the hilt of his sword. "The soldiers... they're closer than I thought."

Ezra stood slowly, his face calm but alert. "How much closer?"

Jonas hesitated, his eyes darting to the mouth of the ravine. "They could be here any moment."

Elijah's blood turned to ice. He rose to his feet, his mind racing. "How did they find us so quickly?"

Jonas didn't answer.

Miriam stood beside Elijah, her eyes narrowing as she looked at Jonas. "Jonas... what's going on?"

For a long moment, Jonas said nothing. The silence stretched, heavy and suffocating, as the truth clawed its way to the surface.

And then, in the distance, the unmistakable sound of boots on stone. Soldiers. Dozens of them, moving quickly, their armor clinking in the still night air.

Elijah's heart pounded in his chest. "You led them here."

Jonas' face twisted with guilt, his voice breaking. "I didn't have a choice."

Miriam stepped forward, her voice rising. "You betrayed us."

"I thought... I thought I could keep them away, buy us time. But—" Jonas stopped, his voice shaking. "I made a deal with one of the soldiers. I was going to lead you to safety in exchange for... for my freedom."

Elijah's vision blurred with rage. "You sold us out."

"I didn't want to," Jonas said, his voice cracking. "But I had to survive."

Before Elijah could respond, the soldiers appeared at the mouth of the ravine, their torches flickering in the darkness, their swords drawn. The group froze, the weight of their impending doom crashing down on them.

"We have to run," Miriam said, her voice sharp with urgency. "Now."

Elijah grabbed the scrolls, his heart pounding in his chest as they scrambled to their feet, the sound of the soldiers' approach growing louder with each passing second.

Jonas stood frozen, his face twisted with regret. "I'm sorry."

Elijah didn't wait for an apology. There was no time. "Come on!" he shouted, pulling Miriam and the others toward the narrow path that led deeper into the ravine.

As they ran, the sound of swords clashing against stone echoed through the air, the soldiers closing in fast.

And behind them, Jonas' voice rang out, a desperate plea in the night.

"I'm sorry."

Act II: Resistance and Preservation

Chapter 4: The Desert Keepers

The desert night was a blanket of stars that stretched endlessly over Qumran, the quiet refuge they had been seeking for days. After the relentless pursuit, the betrayal, and the harsh wilderness, Qumran rose like a whisper of hope from the barren landscape. As Elijah and the others approached, the dark outlines of caves hidden within the mountains became visible—secret, ancient sanctuaries carved into the rocks by hands long gone.

The group moved in silence, their footsteps heavy with exhaustion. Miriam walked beside Elijah, her hand lightly brushing against his arm every so often, as though tethering herself to the only familiarity left in this strange, forsaken world. Behind them, Jonas trailed, his head hung low, a silent ghost of a man. His betrayal was still fresh in their minds, though the chase had left no time for full confrontation.

As they neared the entrance to the community, a soft glow appeared—torchlight, faint but welcoming. Figures moved toward them, cloaked and hooded, the desert wind rustling their robes. Elijah's heart clenched with both anticipation and dread. He knew that they were finally safe from the soldiers, but safety here came with another weight—responsibility.

A tall figure emerged from the group of approaching scholars, his white beard catching the moonlight. His eyes, sharp and probing, fell immediately on Elijah, and the weight of that gaze made Elijah pause.

"You've come a long way," the man said, his voice rough with age but carrying a resonance that stilled the air around them. "Longer than you even know."

Elijah swallowed, his throat dry from the desert, but he spoke clearly. "We carry the sacred scrolls. We've come to protect them, to ensure their survival."

The elder nodded, his eyes gleaming. "I am Abba Nathan, keeper of these scrolls and these people. You are welcome in Qumran." He paused, his gaze lingering on Elijah, as though searching for something deeper. "And you, young man, you carry more than the scrolls. There is a weight on you, a purpose. Come, there is much to discuss."

Inside the cavernous halls of the Qumran caves, the air was cool and damp, a stark contrast to the burning heat of the desert. The walls were lined with shelves—rows upon rows of parchment, each carefully stored in jars, preserved from the harshness of time and the elements. It was a sacred place, an archive of their people's history and faith, hidden away from the world.

As the group settled in, Miriam and the other women were taken to a separate area, where they would rest and help with the daily tasks of the community. The men, including Elijah, were led to a central chamber where Abba Nathan awaited them.

The old scholar sat cross-legged on the floor, his robes pooling around him. He gestured for Elijah to sit across from him, and Elijah did so, feeling the weight of the moment. Jonas remained in the shadows near the entrance, his presence almost invisible, as though he wished he could disappear entirely.

"Elijah," Abba Nathan began, his voice softer now, more thoughtful. "Do you know why you are here?"

Elijah frowned, unsure how to respond. "To protect the scrolls. To preserve the Word of God."

Abba Nathan nodded, but there was a flicker of something else in his eyes—something deeper. "Yes, that is part of it. But you are here because you are part of the prophecy. You, and the scrolls you carry, are part of the greater story of our people's redemption."

Elijah's breath caught in his throat. "Part of the prophecy? How?"

Abba Nathan leaned forward, his eyes sharp and intense. "Isaiah spoke of it, long ago. 'The people walking in darkness have seen a great light; on those living in the land of deep darkness, a light has dawned.'" His voice echoed in the chamber, reverberating off the stone walls. "We are those people, Elijah. We walk in darkness, in the shadow of oppression and destruction. But the light is coming. The Messiah is coming."

Elijah's heart pounded in his chest. The words struck him deeply, filling him with both hope and fear. He had heard the prophecies all his life, but they had always seemed distant, abstract. Now, sitting in the heart of Qumran, with the weight of the scrolls and the ancient wisdom of Abba Nathan surrounding him, the reality of the prophecy felt immediate. Real.

"You believe the Messiah will come soon?" Elijah asked, his voice barely above a whisper.

Abba Nathan smiled, but it was a smile filled with both sorrow and anticipation. "I do. The signs are all around us—the desecration of the temple, the suffering of our people. It is written in the scrolls, and it is written in the heavens. We are living in the days foretold by the prophets."

Elijah's mind raced. If what Abba Nathan said was true, then everything they had endured—the death, the betrayal, the endless journey—was part of something much greater. But the weight of that realization also filled him with dread. What if they failed? What if they couldn't preserve the Word? What if they weren't worthy of this task?

Abba Nathan seemed to sense his unease, for he reached out and placed a hand on Elijah's shoulder. "Do not fear, Elijah. The task before us is great, but we are not alone. The Word has been preserved before, and it will be preserved again. Our job is to ensure that it survives long enough for the Messiah to come and fulfill the prophecies."

Elijah nodded slowly, though his heart still felt heavy. "I don't know if I'm strong enough for this," he admitted, his voice quiet.

Abba Nathan's gaze softened. "Strength does not come from certainty, Elijah. It comes from faith. And faith is often found in the most uncertain of times."

Meanwhile, in a quieter part of the community, Miriam sat among the women of Qumran, her hands busy with the work of preparing food and tending to the needs of the group. The mundane tasks brought a strange sense of peace, a rhythm that allowed her mind to settle, if only for a little while.

But even as her hands worked, her thoughts were far from peaceful. She had fought so hard to bring the scrolls here, to ensure that their mission succeeded. But now that they were in Qumran, surrounded by scholars and the weight of the ancient prophecies, doubts had begun to creep into her heart.

Was this truly what they were meant to do? Would their sacrifices—her brother's death, the loss of Elijah's family, the endless suffering of their people—lead to anything beyond more bloodshed and despair?

That night, after the work was done and the others had gone to sleep, Miriam found Elijah sitting by one of the fires, staring into the flames with a distant look in his eyes.

"Elijah," she said softly, sitting beside him. "What's on your mind?"

He didn't look at her, his gaze fixed on the fire. "I don't know if I can do this, Miriam."

Miriam frowned, surprised by the vulnerability in his voice. Elijah had always been so focused, so determined. To hear him doubt now, after everything they had been through, was unsettling.

"What do you mean?" she asked gently.

Elijah sighed, running a hand through his hair. "Abba Nathan believes that we're part of the prophecy. That the Messiah is coming soon, and that we have to preserve the Word until He arrives. But what if... what if we fail? What if all of this has been for nothing?"

Miriam's heart ached at the uncertainty in his voice, but she understood it all too well. She had been having the same doubts. The same fears. "I've been thinking about that too," she admitted quietly. "We've lost so much, Elijah. Sometimes... sometimes I wonder if it's worth it. If our sacrifices will even matter in the end."

Elijah finally looked at her, his eyes filled with the same uncertainty she felt. "Do you think we're doing the right thing?"

Miriam hesitated, her mind racing. She didn't know if she had an answer. "I think..." she began slowly, choosing her words carefully. "I think that we can't know for sure. But we have to believe that what we're doing is right. That it matters. Because if we don't... then everything we've lost, everything we've sacrificed, really will be for nothing."

Elijah nodded, though the tension in his face didn't ease. "I want to believe that. I do. But it's hard."

Miriam reached out, placing a hand on his arm. "We'll get through this, Elijah. We've made it this far. We just have to keep going."

Jonas stood in the shadows of one of the caves, watching the flickering firelight cast long shadows on the walls. He had been avoiding the others since their arrival, keeping his distance, hoping to fade into the background. But no matter how hard he tried to disappear, the guilt followed him like a shadow he couldn't shake.

His betrayal gnawed at him, a constant reminder of the choices he had made. He had thought he was doing what was necessary to survive, but now, surrounded by the quiet, determined scholars of Qumran, he felt the weight of his actions crushing him.

He glanced over at Miriam and Elijah, watching as they spoke quietly by the fire. They had trusted him. And he had failed them. He had failed all of them.

As the night wore on, Jonas found himself wandering deeper into the caves, away from the others. The air grew cooler, the walls narrowing as he descended into the darkness. His thoughts were a tangled mess of regret, fear, and guilt, and the quiet only amplified the voices in his head.

He stopped suddenly, his hand brushing against the stone wall. His heart pounded in his chest, the weight of everything he had done threatening to overwhelm him.

"I'm sorry," he whispered, though there was no one to hear him. "I'm so sorry."

But no matter how many times he said the words, they didn't change anything. He couldn't undo what he had done.

In the days that followed, life in Qumran settled into a quiet routine. The scholars continued their work, copying the sacred scrolls, preserving the Word for future generations. But beneath the surface, tensions simmered.

Not everyone in the community shared Abba Nathan's vision of preservation. Some argued that survival should be their priority—that they should be focusing on protecting themselves from the ever-present threat of Antiochus' soldiers, not on preserving ancient texts that might never be read.

One evening, as the group gathered for a meal, a heated debate broke out.

"We can't just sit here copying scrolls while our people are being slaughtered!" one of the younger scholars, Benjamin, argued, his voice sharp with frustration. "We should be preparing to fight, to defend ourselves!"

"And what will fighting accomplish?" Abba Nathan replied calmly, his voice steady despite the rising tension. "More bloodshed? More death? The Word is what will survive, not our weapons."

"But what if the Word doesn't survive?" Benjamin shot back, his eyes blazing. "What if we're all killed, and the scrolls are destroyed? What then?"

Abba Nathan's gaze softened, his expression filled with a deep sadness. "The Word has survived centuries of war and destruction. It will survive this too."

Elijah watched the exchange, his heart heavy with the weight of the conversation. He understood Benjamin's frustration—part of him even agreed with it. But he also knew that Abba Nathan was right. The scrolls, the Word, were their only hope. Without them, their people would be lost.

As the debate raged on, Elijah's thoughts drifted to the prophecies. Isaiah 9:2: "The people walking in darkness have seen a great light." He had heard those words countless times, but now they felt different. Now they felt real.

He looked across the table at Abba Nathan, who met his gaze with a knowing smile. The old scholar saw something in him, something Elijah wasn't sure he was ready to acknowledge.

But deep down, Elijah knew that he was part of this. He was part of the prophecy. And whether he liked it or not, he couldn't run from that.

The moon had risen high above Qumran, casting a silvery light over the desert as it lay in a deep, eerie stillness. The scholars who had argued earlier had retreated to their chambers, the tension from the evening still palpable in the cool air. Abba Nathan, ever calm in the face of conflict, had left Elijah with parting words that hung heavy in his mind.

"The Word will survive, Elijah. But survival always comes with sacrifice."

Elijah sat by the fire, his mind racing as the embers flickered in the darkness. Sacrifice. The very word sent a shiver through him. His life had become nothing but a series of sacrifices—his family, his home, his faith. And now, here in Qumran, the weight of the responsibility pressed down on him like never before. Abba Nathan saw him as part of the prophecy, as a crucial piece in the coming of the Messiah. But Elijah couldn't escape the gnawing feeling that something was terribly wrong.

Across from him, Miriam sat quietly, her eyes focused on the flames. She had been distant since their arrival, more so than usual. Elijah could sense the storm of thoughts swirling behind her calm demeanor. She had always been his anchor, his constant through the chaos, but even she seemed to be unraveling under the weight of what they had endured.

"You're still thinking about the argument," she said suddenly, breaking the silence. Her voice was steady, but there was an edge to it that Elijah hadn't noticed before.

He nodded, his gaze still on the fire. "It's hard not to. Benjamin is right in some ways. We can't just sit here and wait for death to come for us."

Miriam's lips tightened, her hands fidgeting with the hem of her cloak. "I've been thinking the same. Abba Nathan's faith is... unshakable. But what if he's wrong? What if we're all wrong?"

Elijah glanced at her, surprised. "You've never doubted before."

Miriam let out a bitter laugh, her eyes darkening. "Haven't I? Elijah, I've doubted every step of this journey. I've questioned everything—God, the prophecies, even our mission here." She looked away, her voice softening. "Especially since Jonas..."

Elijah's stomach twisted at the mention of Jonas. The betrayal was still raw, still festering in the back of his mind. Though Jonas had remained quiet and distant since they had arrived, his presence was like a dark cloud over the group, a constant reminder of the dangers that still lurked outside the walls of Qumran.

"I don't trust him," Elijah said, his voice low. "I can't. Not after what he did."

Miriam's eyes flickered with something—anger? Pain? It was hard to tell. "I don't know if we can trust anyone anymore."

Silence fell between them again, but this time it was heavier, charged with unspoken fears and unresolved tensions. Elijah leaned back, his mind swirling with doubt. The scholars were arguing, the group was fracturing, and his faith, once strong, was now fragile. Could the Messiah really be coming? Could their sacrifices really lead to salvation?

Just as the weight of his thoughts seemed too much to bear, footsteps echoed softly from the cave's entrance. Jonas appeared in the dim light, his face pale, his eyes shadowed with guilt. He stood there for a moment, awkward and uncertain, before speaking.

"Elijah," he said, his voice quiet. "I need to speak with you."

Miriam's eyes narrowed, but she said nothing. Elijah rose slowly, his body tense. He didn't want to hear whatever Jonas had to say, but something in the man's expression—the deep regret, the hollow look in his eyes—kept him from walking away.

"What is it?" Elijah asked, his voice cold.

Jonas shifted uncomfortably, glancing at Miriam before speaking. "It's about the soldiers. The ones who were after us."

Elijah's heart skipped a beat. His mind immediately went to the worst possibilities. Had they found Qumran? Were they closing in on them even now?

"What about them?" Elijah demanded, his tone sharper than he intended.

Jonas hesitated, his hands trembling slightly. "They... they know about Qumran."

Miriam's head snapped up, her eyes wide. "What do you mean, they know?"

Jonas swallowed hard, his face pale as the guilt visibly weighed him down. "When I made the deal to lead them to you back in the ravine, I told them about this place. About the scrolls."

Elijah's world seemed to stop. The air in the cave grew thick, suffocating. His chest tightened, and he felt the blood drain from his face.

"You... what?" Elijah's voice came out as a whisper, full of disbelief.

Jonas' eyes filled with shame. "I didn't mean to. I was desperate. I thought if I gave them this information, they'd let me go, that they'd let us go. But after the ambush failed, I heard rumors that they were planning something. They know about Qumran, Elijah. They're coming for us."

For a long moment, there was nothing but silence. Elijah's mind raced, trying to comprehend what Jonas had just said. He had betrayed them again. After everything they had been through, after the ambush, after bringing them here, Jonas had doomed them all. The soldiers knew about Qumran. Their sanctuary wasn't safe. The scrolls weren't safe.

Miriam stood abruptly, her face livid. "How could you? After everything—after everything, you're still betraying us? You led them here!"

Jonas shook his head desperately. "No, I didn't lead them here. I didn't—"

"Then what do you call this?" Miriam demanded, her voice rising. "You gave them this place! They'll come, and they'll destroy everything. They'll kill us all!"

Jonas' face crumpled, his voice breaking. "I didn't mean for it to happen like this. I thought... I thought I could fix it. I thought I could protect you."

"Protect us?" Elijah's voice was cold, dark with fury. He stepped forward, his fists clenched at his sides. "You've condemned us."

Jonas took a step back, fear flashing in his eyes. "Please, Elijah, you have to believe me. I didn't know it would come to this."

Elijah's hands shook with anger, his vision blurred with the overwhelming weight of betrayal. But before he could speak, before he could unleash the torrent of rage building inside him, Abba Nathan appeared in the entrance to the chamber, his face solemn.

"What's happening here?" the elder asked, his calm voice a stark contrast to the tension filling the cave.

Miriam turned to him, her voice quivering with fury. "Jonas has doomed us. The soldiers are coming. He told them about Qumran."

Abba Nathan's expression didn't change, though his eyes darkened with understanding. He looked at Jonas for a long, silent moment, as though weighing the truth in his heart.

Jonas stood trembling, his hands clutching at his sides. "I'm sorry. I didn't mean for it to happen. But... but they're coming."

Abba Nathan closed his eyes, sighing deeply. "It seems our time has come sooner than I expected."

Elijah's chest tightened. "What do we do?"

For the first time, Abba Nathan's calm façade faltered. He looked out into the night, his eyes distant, his voice heavy with sorrow. "We do what we've always done, Elijah. We protect the Word. But we must be prepared to face the darkness before the light can come."

Elijah's stomach churned. The scrolls, the prophecies—everything they had worked to preserve—were at risk. If the soldiers found them, all of it would be lost. The Messiah's coming, the fulfillment of Isaiah's prophecy—it would all be in vain.

"What about the scrolls?" Miriam asked, her voice breaking. "What do we do with them?"

Abba Nathan turned to her, his expression grave. "We hide them. Deep in the caves, where no one can find them. The Word will survive, even if we don't."

The words hung in the air, heavy and final. Elijah's heart pounded in his chest. Abba Nathan's calm acceptance of their fate shook him to his core. Was this really the end? Were they to die here, in the desert, with nothing but the scrolls buried deep in the ground?

Abba Nathan's gaze shifted to Elijah, his eyes filled with something deeper than words could express. "This is your task, Elijah. You must ensure the Word survives. The scrolls must be hidden, protected. And if the soldiers come... you must be prepared to give your life to protect them."

Elijah's breath caught in his throat. He had known, somewhere deep down, that this might be his fate. But hearing it spoken so plainly, so directly, shook him. He wasn't ready for this. He wasn't ready to die. Not yet.

"What about the others?" Elijah asked, his voice trembling. "What about Miriam, and Jonas, and the rest of the scholars?"

Abba Nathan's face softened. "They will do what they must. We all will. But your task is the most important, Elijah. The Word must survive."

Elijah looked at Miriam, her face pale but resolute. She had been his constant, his strength, through all of this. Could he really leave her behind? Could he sacrifice himself for the scrolls, knowing what it would mean for her?

Abba Nathan stepped forward, placing a hand on Elijah's shoulder. "You are part of the prophecy, Elijah. The people walking in darkness have seen a great light. You are that light, even if you cannot see it yet."

Elijah's heart pounded, his mind racing. The weight of the prophecy, of the responsibility, felt like too much. But there was no other choice. The soldiers were coming. They had to protect the Word.

"I'll do it," Elijah said, his voice barely above a whisper. "I'll hide the scrolls."

Abba Nathan smiled sadly, his eyes filled with both pride and sorrow. "I knew you would."

As the group prepared to move the scrolls deeper into the caves, Elijah couldn't shake the feeling that this was the beginning of the end. The soldiers were coming, and everything they had fought for, everything they had sacrificed, hung in the balance.

But deep down, beneath the fear, beneath the doubt, there was a flicker of something. A flicker of hope.

The Word would survive. No matter what.

Chapter 5: Secrets in the Caves

The caves of Qumran had become a world unto themselves, a refuge from the burning sun and a sanctuary from the violence that continued to ravage Jerusalem. Here, beneath the earth, where the light barely touched the stone walls, Elijah and the scribes worked tirelessly. The scrolls lay before them like fragile treasures, each one a sacred link between their past and the future that hung in uncertainty.

Elijah's hands were blistered and cracked, his eyes bloodshot from sleepless nights spent transcribing the ancient words. He was no longer just copying them—he was absorbing them, drinking in every syllable as though they were sustenance for his soul. The words of Micah 5:2, in particular, had gripped him in a way that nothing else had before: "But you, Bethlehem Ephrathah, though you are small among the clans of Judah, out of you will come for me one who will be ruler over Israel, whose origins are from of old, from ancient times."

He had read the prophecy dozens of times now, each reading deeper than the last. It was no longer just a prediction—it was a beacon in the darkness. Bethlehem. The Messiah would come from Bethlehem. Elijah could see it as clearly as the ink drying on the parchment before him. The Messiah would not come as a warrior king to crush their enemies but as something different, something more.

Still, as Elijah continued to immerse himself in the prophecies, he found his mind being pulled in another direction—toward Isaiah 53, the prophecy of the suffering servant. It had always been a mystery to him and to many of the scholars. But now, in the dim light of the caves, something in those words tugged at his soul.

"He was despised and rejected by men, a man of sorrows, and familiar with suffering. Like one from whom men hide their faces he was despised, and we esteemed him not."

The suffering servant. The Messiah would suffer.

The thought gnawed at Elijah, unsettling him. Could the Messiah, the long-awaited Redeemer of Israel, truly be destined to suffer? Was their salvation tied not to a triumphant king but to a man who would bear the weight of their sins, who would be crushed for their iniquities? It was almost too much to comprehend, and yet, the more he read, the more convinced he became that this was the truth.

"Elijah," a voice broke through the stillness, pulling him from his thoughts. Miriam stood at the entrance of the cave, her brow creased with concern. She had been making more and more trips back to Jerusalem, slipping through the cracks in the city's defenses to aid the resistance. Her role in the rebellion was growing, and though she returned to Qumran, Elijah could sense that her heart was still in the fight. She had been distant lately, her once steady presence now a flicker that came and went like the wind.

"You haven't eaten," Miriam said, stepping closer. She was wearing the dark, tattered cloak she used for her trips into the city, her face smeared with dirt and exhaustion. "You've been down here for hours."

Elijah blinked, as though just realizing the passage of time. He glanced around the cave, the faint light of the torches flickering on the stone walls, the sound of scribes murmuring in the background as they worked.

"I lost track," he muttered, running a hand through his hair, which had grown longer and more unkempt during their time in Qumran. "There's too much to do."

Miriam crouched beside him, her eyes scanning the scrolls spread out before him. "You're fixated, Elijah. You're not just copying these words anymore. You're living in them."

Elijah frowned, the weight of her words pressing against his chest. He knew she was right. He had become consumed by the prophecies, by the mystery of the Messiah's coming, and it was pulling him further away from everything—and everyone—around him. But he couldn't stop. The scrolls called to him, the words demanding his attention, his understanding. There was something there, hidden between the lines, something that would reveal itself if he just dug deep enough.

"Don't you see, Miriam?" he said, his voice hoarse with desperation. "The Messiah... He's coming. But He's not what we think He is. He's not going to come with armies and swords. He's going to suffer."

Miriam's face tightened, her eyes narrowing as she studied him. "You're talking about Isaiah 53."

"Yes," Elijah said, the word spilling out like a confession. "The suffering servant. That's what the Messiah will be. He'll suffer for us, Miriam. He'll be crushed, but through His suffering, we'll be saved."

Miriam shook her head slowly, disbelief flashing across her face. "You sound like you're losing yourself in this. We've always believed the Messiah would deliver us from our enemies, that He'd restore Israel to its former glory. Now you're saying He'll suffer? That He'll be crushed?"

"I know it sounds impossible," Elijah said, his voice rising. "But look at the prophecies. Micah speaks of His birth in Bethlehem, but Isaiah speaks of His suffering. It's all there, if you just look."

Miriam's gaze softened, but her concern didn't fade. "Elijah, I've been back in Jerusalem. I've seen what Antiochus' soldiers are doing to our people. They're slaughtering us. They're destroying everything. We need a king—a warrior—to save us. Not a man destined to suffer."

Elijah's chest tightened with frustration. She didn't understand. No one did. They were all still clinging to the old hopes of a political savior, a Messiah who would come in glory and power. But that wasn't what the prophecies were telling him.

"Don't you see?" Elijah said, his voice thick with urgency. "It's not about swords or armies. It's about something deeper. Redemption. It's not just for Israel—it's for all of us."

Miriam stood slowly, her eyes hardening. "I'm going back to Jerusalem soon. The resistance needs me." She hesitated, her voice dropping. "I thought... I thought we were in this together, Elijah. But you're slipping away. You're losing yourself in these prophecies, and I don't know if I can follow you there."

Elijah opened his mouth to speak, but the words wouldn't come. He watched as Miriam turned and walked out of the cave, her figure disappearing into the shadows. She had been his anchor, his strength, and now she was slipping away, drawn back to the chaos of the city while he remained buried in the scrolls.

As the days passed, Elijah delved deeper into the prophecies, particularly Isaiah 53. His mind became consumed with the image of the suffering servant, of a Messiah who would bear the sins of the people. The other scribes noticed his growing obsession, but they said nothing, allowing him to work in silence. The deeper he went, the more the words of Isaiah echoed in his mind, as though they were calling to him from some distant place:

"He was pierced for our transgressions, he was crushed for our iniquities; the punishment that brought us peace was on him, and by his wounds we are healed."

The words haunted him, pulling him further from the world around him. Each line spoke of pain, of sacrifice, of a love so profound it could only come from God. But the suffering... how could their Messiah, their promised Deliverer, be destined for such agony?

Elijah found himself scribbling notes furiously beside the scrolls, trying to piece together the puzzle of the Messiah's coming. He no longer slept, his mind racing through the nights, consumed with visions of a man bloodied and broken, carrying the weight of the world's sins on His shoulders. He could see it in his mind—the Messiah walking to His death, His body ravaged by pain, but in His suffering, a light shone. A light that would save them all.

Meanwhile, Jonas had been growing more distant. Though he remained in Qumran, helping the scholars as best he could, his internal struggle had reached a breaking point. His guilt over the betrayal still weighed on him, and though no one had spoken of it directly since they'd learned of the soldiers' pursuit, he could feel the tension between him and the others like a living thing.

He had thought he could protect them, that by feeding small bits of information to Antiochus' soldiers, he could delay their pursuit, buy the group more time. But as the days wore on, the weight of his deception gnawed at him like a festering wound. Each day he saw Elijah, Miriam, and the others working tirelessly to preserve the sacred scrolls, he felt like more of a traitor.

He was protecting them, wasn't he? By feeding false leads to the soldiers, wasn't he ensuring that the group remained hidden? That the scrolls remained safe? But deep down, Jonas knew that no amount of rationalization could ease his conscience. He had betrayed them. He had doomed them all. It was only a matter of time before the soldiers closed in.

Jonas sat in the shadows of the cave one night, his mind a whirlwind of guilt and fear. He had to do something—something to make it right. But what could he do? If the soldiers arrived at Qumran, he would be to blame. And if they never came, his betrayal would still hang over him like a curse.

As he stared into the darkness, his heart racing with dread, the echo of his own voice whispered in his mind: I'm sorry. I'm sorry. I'm sorry.

The tension within the group grew as Elijah became more withdrawn. His obsession with the suffering servant prophecy had alienated him from the others, and even Abba Nathan, who had once viewed Elijah as a critical part of the prophecy, began to worry that the young scribe was losing himself in the scriptures.

One evening, as Elijah sat alone in the deepest part of the cave, surrounded by scrolls and fragments of parchment, Abba Nathan approached him. The elder's eyes were kind but filled with concern.

"Elijah," Abba Nathan said softly, sitting beside him. "You've been working tirelessly, but I fear you are losing sight of yourself. The prophecies are important, yes, but they are not everything."

Elijah's hands tightened around the scroll he had been studying. "Don't you see, Abba? The Messiah... He will suffer. He will die for us. It's right here, in the words of Isaiah. How can we ignore that?"

Abba Nathan's brow furrowed. "I do not deny the prophecy, Elijah. But you must not lose yourself in it. The Messiah's coming is about more than suffering. It is about redemption, about hope. You have become fixated on the pain, but there is light beyond the darkness."

Elijah stared at him, his heart pounding. "How can there be light without the suffering? How can we be saved without the Messiah's sacrifice?"

Abba Nathan placed a hand on Elijah's shoulder, his voice gentle but firm. "You are not meant to carry the weight of the prophecy alone, Elijah. The Messiah's suffering is not yours to bear. You must have faith that the light will come, even if you cannot see it now."

Elijah felt a lump form in his throat, the weight of his obsession pressing down on him like a crushing force. He had been so consumed with the suffering, with the idea of a Messiah who would die for them, that he had forgotten about the hope that lay beyond that sacrifice. But even as Abba Nathan's words soothed his heart, a part of Elijah still clung to the prophecy. The suffering was real. The pain was real. And it was coming.

Elijah sat in silence long after Abba Nathan had left. His mentor's words echoed in the stillness of the cave, yet they did little to soothe the storm within him. How could he believe in hope when the path ahead was paved with suffering? The words of Isaiah were etched deep into his soul, and now they haunted him, filling his thoughts with images of a broken Messiah, despised and rejected by the very people He had come to save.

But beyond the suffering, Elijah sensed something else—something he couldn't yet name. It was as though the light Abba Nathan spoke of lay just beyond his reach, hidden in the shadows of the prophecies. And that uncertainty, that feeling of teetering on the edge of a revelation he could not yet grasp, gnawed at him.

Footsteps echoed down the narrow corridor of the cave, drawing his attention. A figure emerged from the darkness, cloaked in shadows but unmistakable—Miriam.

She had returned from Jerusalem, her face streaked with dirt, her body weary from the long journey. But there was something else in her eyes this time—something Elijah hadn't seen before. A weight, heavier than the exhaustion of travel.

"Elijah," she said quietly, her voice soft but edged with something sharp. "We need to talk."

He rose from his place on the cold stone floor, his eyes searching hers. "What is it? What's happened?"

Miriam hesitated for a moment, then stepped closer, lowering her voice. "The resistance in Jerusalem… it's not going as we hoped. The people are fighting, but it's chaos. There's no unity, no leadership. The soldiers are tightening their grip on the city. And…" Her voice faltered, and she looked away, as if struggling to find the words.

Elijah's heart sank. "And what?"

Miriam's gaze met his, her eyes dark with pain. "There's been talk. Rumors, mostly. But people are starting to doubt the prophecies. Some believe the Messiah isn't coming at all. They say we've been abandoned. That we're fools for holding on to hope when everything is crumbling around us."

Elijah felt a chill run down his spine. Abandoned. The word clung to him, feeding the doubt that had already begun to fester in his mind. Were they fools for believing in a Messiah who would come to save them? For clinging to ancient words written on fragile scrolls while the world outside collapsed?

"I don't know what to believe anymore," Miriam continued, her voice trembling. "I want to believe in the prophecies. I want to believe that we're part of something greater. But I've seen what's happening in Jerusalem. I've seen the suffering. And it's hard, Elijah. It's hard to hold on."

Elijah's hands tightened into fists at his sides. He could feel the tension between them, the widening chasm that the prophecies and their own experiences had opened. Miriam had always been his grounding force, the one who kept him tethered to the world, to reality. But now, she was slipping away, caught in the same storm of doubt that plagued him.

"We can't give up, Miriam," he said, though his voice lacked the conviction he wished it held. "The Messiah will come. I know it."

Miriam shook her head, tears glistening in her eyes. "How do you know that, Elijah? How can you be so sure?"

Because the prophecies say so. The words were on the tip of his tongue, but they felt hollow. He couldn't explain how he knew—he just did. Yet how could he expect Miriam to believe when he, himself, was beginning to doubt?

Before he could answer, another figure appeared in the cave entrance—Jonas. His face was pale, his eyes wide with fear.

"They're coming," he said, his voice breathless. "The soldiers. They're on their way."

Elijah and Miriam turned to him, the weight of his words sinking in like a stone dropping into a well.

"How do you know?" Miriam demanded, her voice sharp.

Jonas swallowed, his gaze darting nervously between them. "I overheard some of the men talking before I left Jerusalem. They were planning a raid. Qumran isn't safe anymore."

Elijah's stomach dropped. The soldiers were coming. Everything they had worked for—everything they had risked—was now in danger. The scrolls, the sacred words, could be lost.

"How much time do we have?" Elijah asked, his voice tight.

Jonas shook his head. "Not much. A few days, maybe. But if we don't move the scrolls now, they'll find them."

Panic surged through Elijah. The scrolls—the sacred texts that had survived centuries of war, exile, and oppression—were about to be destroyed, wiped from existence by Antiochus' men. All their efforts, all the sacrifices they had made, would be for nothing.

"We need to hide them," Elijah said, his mind racing. "Deep in the caves, somewhere they'll never find."

Miriam's face was pale, her eyes wide with fear. "Where? There's not enough time."

Elijah turned to Jonas, his chest tight with urgency. "Do you know the caves well enough to find a place?"

Jonas hesitated, his face filled with guilt. He had betrayed them once, led the soldiers to their door, and now the consequences of that betrayal were closing in on them. But in this moment, there was no room for second chances. They had to act.

"I'll help you," Jonas said finally, his voice shaking. "I owe you that much."

Elijah nodded, though the bitterness in his heart lingered. Jonas had caused this, and now he would help fix it. But it wasn't forgiveness that drove Elijah—it was desperation.

As night fell, Elijah, Jonas, and a small group of scribes moved quickly through the caves, carrying the most sacred scrolls deeper into the mountains. They moved silently, their torches flickering in the darkness as they descended into the deepest parts of the cave system, where the air was thin and cold.

Elijah led the way, his mind focused on one thing—preserving the Word. The suffering servant, the Messiah, the prophecies—they had to survive, even if he didn't. He would hide the scrolls, bury them so deep that no soldier, no enemy, could ever find them.

Behind him, Jonas walked in silence, the weight of his guilt pressing down on him like a physical force. Every step he took felt like another stone added to the burden on his shoulders. He had betrayed them once, and now the soldiers were coming to finish what he had started. But this time, Jonas swore he would make it right. He would help Elijah save the scrolls, even if it cost him his life.

They reached a narrow passageway that opened into a small cavern, hidden deep within the heart of the mountain. The air was damp, the walls lined with ancient stone carvings that spoke of a time long before their own.

"This is it," Elijah said, his voice echoing in the darkness. "This is where we'll hide them."

One by one, the scribes began placing the scrolls into large earthen jars, sealing them tightly before burying them in the deepest parts of the cavern. Elijah worked alongside them, his hands steady despite the weight of the moment. These scrolls were more than just parchment and ink—they were the lifeblood of their people, the key to their redemption. They could not be lost.

As they finished burying the last of the scrolls, Elijah stood back, his chest heaving with exhaustion. It was done. The Word was hidden, protected. But the fear that had gripped him from the moment Jonas had warned them still lingered.

"They'll never find them here," Jonas said quietly, his voice thick with emotion. "I swear it."

Elijah turned to him, his eyes hard. "You'd better be right."

Jonas nodded, though the guilt in his eyes was unmistakable. "I am."

But as they made their way back through the narrow passageways, Elijah couldn't shake the feeling that this was only the beginning. The soldiers were coming, and soon the caves would no longer be a refuge. Their sanctuary had been compromised, and now they were running out of time.

The prophecies had foretold of suffering, of pain, but also of redemption. Elijah clung to that promise, even as doubt gnawed at his heart. The Messiah would come. He had to. Because if He didn't, everything they had fought for, everything they had sacrificed, would be in vain.

As the last of the torches flickered and died, leaving them in darkness, Elijah whispered a silent prayer into the void, his voice trembling with desperation.

"Let the Word survive. Let it be enough."

The weight of the scrolls lingered in Elijah's thoughts even as they made their way back from the cavern. His mind was a swirling chaos of scripture and fear, prophecy and reality. The deeper they went into hiding the scrolls, the more deeply buried he felt. The stones of Qumran seemed to press in on him, each one whispering ancient words that had been forgotten by time but were now engraved into his soul. The night was thick around them as they returned to the main chamber, but despite the completion of their task, Elijah's heart was not eased.

As they neared the central cave, the faint murmur of voices echoed ahead. Elijah recognized Abba Nathan's voice, calm and measured, speaking to the group of scribes and scholars who remained in Qumran. His voice carried a weight of authority but also a gentle reassurance that seemed to stand firm, even in the face of impending danger.

Elijah, Jonas, and the others entered the chamber to find Abba Nathan standing at the center of a small gathering. Miriam was there too, sitting at the edge of the fire, her face set in quiet reflection. She looked up as they entered, but Elijah noticed her eyes quickly drop away from his. Something had changed between them, and it felt like an unspoken wall had risen between them, built of doubt and distance.

"We have done what we can," Abba Nathan said, looking toward Elijah and Jonas as they approached. "The Word is hidden, safe for now. But we are not safe, not yet. The soldiers of Antiochus will come, and they will search these caves. But they will find only stone and shadows."

There was a murmur among the group, a mixture of relief and fear. Abba Nathan's words were meant to comfort them, but the looming threat was too great to ignore. Each person knew that the days ahead would be perilous, and survival was not guaranteed.

Elijah moved toward Abba Nathan, his voice low. "We hid the scrolls as far into the caves as we could. But if the soldiers search thoroughly enough..."

Abba Nathan raised a hand, his face calm. "Do not let fear guide your thoughts, Elijah. You have done all that was required of you. The rest is in the hands of God."

Elijah wanted to believe that. He wanted to believe that, by some divine miracle, the scrolls would remain untouched, hidden from those who sought to destroy them. But the weight of the prophecies, the suffering servant of Isaiah 53, filled his mind with visions of the worst. Suffering. Betrayal. Destruction. What if it wasn't just the Messiah who would suffer? What if it was all of them?

Abba Nathan's eyes lingered on Elijah for a moment, as though sensing the turmoil that boiled beneath the surface. "You are carrying more than your share of the burden, my son," the elder said softly. "The prophecies speak of suffering, yes. But they also speak of light. Redemption. You must remember that."

Elijah nodded, though the words felt hollow. He had heard Abba Nathan's reassurances before, but each time they felt further away, less tangible, like grasping at smoke. The Messiah was coming—that much Elijah was certain of—but what would that truly mean for them? Would His arrival come with hope, or would it be heralded by a wave of destruction?

Miriam stood, her eyes shifting between Abba Nathan and Elijah. Her movements were quiet, measured, as though she were navigating some unseen divide. She took a breath before she spoke, her voice carefully controlled. "I need to return to Jerusalem soon."

Elijah turned to her, surprise flickering across his face. "So soon? You just got back."

"I have to go back," she replied, her voice firm. "The resistance needs me, and there's more work to be done. They need supplies, and they need someone they can trust."

Elijah's heart sank. He wanted to ask her to stay, to stay here with him, with the group, where they could continue their work together. But something about the way she spoke, the way her eyes seemed to avoid his, told him that she had already made her decision. Her place wasn't here—not anymore.

"We need you here, too," Elijah said softly, though he knew the words were futile.

Miriam shook her head. "You don't need me, Elijah. You have the scrolls, the prophecies. That's your mission. But mine..." She paused, her voice softening. "My mission is out there. With the people who are still fighting."

There was an unspoken pain in her words, a subtle accusation that Elijah couldn't ignore. She was still grounded in the fight for survival, for their people, while he had become lost in the words of the ancient scrolls. She was right, and yet, he couldn't abandon what he had come to believe. The Messiah's arrival was the only thing that mattered. But that belief had driven a wedge between them, one that might never be removed.

Miriam looked at Abba Nathan, her expression resolute. "I'll leave in the morning."

The elder nodded, his face sad but understanding. "Go with God, Miriam. May He guide your steps."

Elijah's chest tightened as he watched her walk away, disappearing into the shadows of the cave. The silence that followed felt heavy, like an unspoken farewell that lingered in the air. He wanted to follow her, to say something, anything, that would make her stay, but he remained rooted in place, unable to move.

As the night deepened, Elijah retreated to a secluded corner of the cave, the scrolls spread out before him like a comforting shroud. He read the words of Isaiah 53 once again, but now, the prophecy felt more personal, more pressing. The suffering servant was not just a distant figure in a future that had yet to unfold—He was a mirror of Elijah's own struggle. The weight of sacrifice, the burden of carrying a truth that few understood.

"He was oppressed and afflicted, yet he did not open his mouth; he was led like a lamb to the slaughter, and as a sheep before its shearers is silent, so he did not open his mouth."

Elijah closed his eyes, the words cutting deep. He could feel the pain in them, the quiet suffering of a man who would bear the sins of others, who would walk willingly into darkness so that others might find the light. Was that his role, too? Was he destined to carry this burden in silence, while others fought and struggled in the world outside?

The sound of footsteps echoed down the passageway, breaking Elijah from his thoughts. He looked up to see Jonas standing at the entrance, his face pale and drawn.

"Elijah," Jonas said quietly, his voice shaking. "We need to talk."

Elijah frowned, rising to his feet. "What is it? Have the soldiers—"

"No, it's not that," Jonas interrupted, his hands trembling as he spoke. "It's... it's about Miriam."

Elijah's heart skipped a beat, dread flooding his chest. "What about Miriam?"

Jonas hesitated, his eyes filled with guilt and fear. "She's... she's walking into a trap. The soldiers—they know she's been helping the resistance. They're waiting for her in Jerusalem."

Elijah's breath caught in his throat. "What? How do you know this?"

"I overheard them talking," Jonas admitted, his voice cracking. "Back when I... when I was feeding them information. They know about her. They know everything. If she goes back to the city, they'll take her."

Elijah felt his world tilt, his mind racing. Miriam was walking into a death trap, and she didn't even know it. All this time, while he had been consumed by the prophecies, by the words of Isaiah, she had been risking her life for something tangible, something real. And now, her life hung in the balance.

"We have to stop her," Elijah said, his voice trembling with urgency. "We have to warn her before she leaves."

Jonas nodded, though the guilt in his eyes remained. "I'll help you. I owe her that."

Elijah didn't hesitate. He rushed down the passageway, his heart pounding as he searched for Miriam. The words of the prophecies swirled in his mind, but now they felt distant, overshadowed by the pressing reality of the moment. The suffering servant, the Messiah's coming—it all faded into the background as a single, overpowering thought consumed him.

He had to save her.

They found her near the entrance to the caves, preparing for her journey. The sky above had begun to lighten with the first hints of dawn, casting the desert in soft, muted colors. Miriam was fastening the strap of a small satchel to her side when she heard Elijah's approach.

"Miriam!" Elijah called out, his voice tight with panic.

She turned to him, surprise flashing across her face. "Elijah, what—"

"You can't go back to Jerusalem," he said, breathless as he reached her. "The soldiers... they know about you. They're waiting."

Miriam's eyes widened, her body going still. "What are you talking about?"

"Jonas overheard them," Elijah said, glancing at Jonas, who stood behind him, his face pale with guilt. "They know you've been helping the resistance. If you go back, they'll take you."

Miriam stared at him, her expression unreadable. For a moment, Elijah thought she might argue, might insist on going despite the danger. But then, slowly, her shoulders sagged, and she closed her eyes.

"I see," she said softly, her voice barely a whisper.

Elijah stepped closer, his heart pounding. "You can't go, Miriam. Not now. Not like this."

She opened her eyes, and for the first time in what felt like days, she looked directly at him, her gaze steady and full of unspoken words. "And what am I supposed to do, Elijah? Stay here? Hide away while others fight and die?"

"I don't know," he admitted, his voice breaking. "But I can't lose you. Not like this."

Miriam's eyes softened, and for a brief moment, the distance between them seemed to shrink. But then, just as quickly, it returned, the weight of their choices, their paths, pulling them apart once more.

"I'm not staying here forever," she said quietly. "But for now... I'll wait."

Elijah let out a breath he hadn't realized he'd been holding. The danger had been averted, at least for now, but the threat still loomed. The soldiers would come, and Miriam's heart still longed to return to the fight.

But for now, they had each other. And for now, that would have to be enough.

Chapter 6: The Growing Expectation

The sky over Qumran was bruised with the colors of dusk, the horizon a dim line that faded into the endless desert. The quiet that had once felt like a refuge now pressed in on the small group of scribes and scholars, each of them haunted by the growing weight of their mission. The scrolls were hidden, but the soldiers of Antiochus were closing in, their presence a dark shadow that stretched from Jerusalem to the desert caves.

Elijah sat alone near the entrance to one of the caves, the wind stirring the dust around him as he stared out at the horizon. His thoughts were consumed by the prophecies, his heart wrapped tightly around the words of Isaiah. The suffering servant. He had read the passage so many times now that it felt like part of him, its message seeping into his bones.

"He was oppressed and afflicted, yet he did not open his mouth; he was led like a lamb to the slaughter, and as a sheep before its shearers is silent, so he did not open his mouth."

Elijah could feel the prophecy unfolding, not just in his mind, but in the world around him. The suffering was all too real. The oppression. The affliction. It was everywhere, from the streets of Jerusalem to the hidden caves of Qumran. But where was the light that Isaiah had spoken of? Where was the redemption that was supposed to come through the suffering?

His thoughts were interrupted by the soft shuffle of footsteps behind him. He turned to see Ezra approaching, his face lined with years of wisdom and sorrow. The elder had always carried the weight of their mission with grace, but lately, even Ezra seemed burdened by the darkness that hung over them all.

"Elijah," Ezra said, sitting down beside him, his voice soft. "You've been distant."

"I've been thinking," Elijah replied, his voice quiet. "About the prophecies. About what they mean for us. For all of us."

Ezra nodded slowly, his gaze shifting to the horizon. "The prophecies are difficult to understand, especially in times like these. But they are also a source of hope. Even in the midst of suffering, there is hope."

Elijah's chest tightened. "I don't know if I see it anymore, Ezra. The suffering servant, the Messiah—what if He doesn't come? What if we're wrong? What if all of this... everything we've done... is for nothing?"

Ezra turned to him, his eyes filled with compassion. "I've asked myself the same questions. But the Word, Elijah, the prophecies—they are not just words on parchment. They are the voice of God. And that voice tells us that the Messiah will come, even if we don't yet understand how or when."

Elijah wanted to believe him, to hold on to the hope that had sustained them through so much. But doubt gnawed at him, especially as the weight of their mission grew heavier with each passing day. How could he trust in a future he couldn't see, in a prophecy that seemed to promise more suffering?

Ezra smiled softly, sensing Elijah's turmoil. "You have done well, Elijah. You have carried this burden with more strength than you know. But remember, the suffering is not the end. It is only the beginning."

The quiet of Qumran shattered suddenly that night. It began with the sound of metal on stone, the clang of swords in the distance. Elijah jerked awake from a restless sleep, his heart pounding. He bolted upright, his senses on high alert. It was a sound that didn't belong here, not in this sacred place.

The scholars and scribes were already stirring, their eyes wide with fear. Miriam, who had been sleeping near the entrance of the cave, was on her feet, her face pale as she scanned the darkness beyond the cave's mouth.

"Elijah," she whispered, her voice trembling. "Something's wrong."

Before Elijah could respond, the sound grew louder—shouts, the unmistakable sound of soldiers approaching. Panic surged through the group, and Elijah felt his blood turn cold. The soldiers had found them.

"Get the scrolls," someone yelled, but Elijah knew there wasn't time. The scrolls were hidden deep in the caves, but the soldiers wouldn't care about the texts. They were here for them—the people.

The next moments were a blur. Soldiers burst into the cave, their torches casting flickering shadows against the walls. Shouts echoed through the chamber as the scholars scrambled to escape, but there was nowhere to go. The narrow passages that had once been their sanctuary now felt like a death trap.

Elijah grabbed Miriam's arm, pulling her toward the back of the cave as chaos erupted around them. Ezra was trying to calm the others, his voice steady even as the soldiers closed in. But Elijah knew there was no reasoning with them. They had come to destroy.

The first clash of swords rang out, and Elijah felt his stomach drop. He had never seen death so close, never felt the heat of battle press against his skin like this. And then, in an instant, everything changed.

A soldier struck out at Ezra, his sword slicing through the air with deadly precision. Elijah watched in horror as the blade connected, as Ezra fell to the ground, his blood pooling beneath him. The elder's face was pale, his eyes wide with shock, but there was no time for words, no time for anything.

"Elijah!" Miriam screamed, pulling him away from the scene as another soldier advanced toward them. They ducked into a narrow passage, the sound of battle ringing in their ears as they fled deeper into the caves.

Elijah's heart pounded in his chest, his mind reeling from the sight of Ezra's lifeless body. The elder, the man who had been their guide, their leader, was gone. And with him, it felt as though the very foundation of their mission had crumbled.

The raid lasted for what felt like hours, though in reality it was only minutes. The soldiers tore through Qumran, destroying everything in their path. Several of the scrolls were lost, their pages scattered and burned. By the time the soldiers left, the caves were littered with the dead.

Elijah stood among the wreckage, his body trembling with exhaustion and grief. He could barely comprehend what had happened, the devastation that had been wrought in such a short time. Ezra was gone. Several of the scribes had been killed. And the scrolls—so many of the sacred texts they had worked to preserve—were destroyed.

Miriam sat against the wall, her face pale as she clutched her side, blood seeping through her fingers. She had been injured during the raid, but in the chaos, Elijah hadn't even noticed. Now, seeing her like this, the weight of everything crashed down on him.

He knelt beside her, his heart aching with guilt. "Miriam, I'm so sorry. I didn't... I didn't protect you. I didn't protect any of them."

Miriam's eyes flickered open, her breath shallow but steady. "This isn't your fault, Elijah," she whispered, her voice strained. "We all knew the risks."

"But Ezra... the scrolls..." Elijah's voice broke, his grief spilling out in waves. "I failed. I failed all of you."

Miriam's hand reached out, her fingers weak but steady as they touched his arm. "You didn't fail. You're still here. And the scrolls—they aren't all lost. Some of them survived."

Elijah swallowed hard, his throat tight. "But what does it matter? We've lost so much. How can we continue?"

Miriam's eyes closed for a moment, her breath labored. "Because we have to. Because the prophecies aren't just about the past, Elijah. They're about the future. The Messiah is coming. We have to believe that."

Elijah's heart twisted with pain. He had believed once, so strongly, so fiercely. But now, with Ezra gone, with so much of their work destroyed, how could he still believe?

As if sensing his thoughts, Miriam's voice softened. "Elijah, you've carried this burden for so long. But you're not alone. We're still here. We can still fight."

Elijah looked at her, his chest tightening with emotion. Despite her injuries, despite everything that had happened, Miriam still had hope. And in that moment, Elijah realized that hope was all they had left.

In the days that followed, the survivors of Qumran tried to rebuild. They mourned the loss of Ezra and the others who had died in the raid, their grief a heavy shroud that covered the entire group. The remaining scrolls were gathered and hidden once more, though the loss of so many sacred texts weighed heavily on Elijah's heart.

Jonas was nowhere to be found. He had fled during the raid, consumed by guilt and fear. Elijah hadn't seen him since the attack, and part of him wasn't sure if he ever wanted to see Jonas again. The betrayal had been too great, the cost too high.

But as the days passed, Elijah couldn't help but wonder if Jonas had fled for another reason. Perhaps the guilt had finally driven him to seek redemption, to find some way to atone for the destruction he had caused. Elijah didn't know, but part of him hoped that Jonas would find his way back, that somehow, there could still be forgiveness.

Miriam's injuries slowly began to heal, though the emotional wounds lingered. She became quieter, more withdrawn, as though the weight of survival had pressed down on her too heavily. Elijah tried to comfort her, but there was little he could do. The grief was too fresh, too raw.

One night, as they sat together in the quiet of the caves, Miriam finally spoke.

"Do you think… do you think the Messiah will really come?" she asked, her voice barely above a whisper.

Elijah didn't answer immediately. The words of Isaiah 53 still echoed in his mind, the image of the suffering servant more vivid than ever. He had once believed so strongly in the coming of the Messiah, in the promise of redemption. But now, that belief felt distant, like a dream that had slipped through his fingers.

"I don't know," Elijah admitted, his voice soft. "But I have to believe that He will. Otherwise, what's the point of all this?"

Miriam nodded, though her eyes remained fixed on the darkness beyond the cave. "I want to believe too. But sometimes… sometimes it's hard."

Elijah reached out, his hand covering hers. "We'll keep fighting. We'll keep preserving the Word. And when the time comes, the Messiah will come. I have to believe that."

Miriam's gaze finally met his, her eyes filled with a mixture of hope and sorrow. "And if He doesn't?"

Elijah's heart ached at the question, but he forced himself to smile. "Then we'll keep fighting anyway."

The days following the raid on Qumran were a blur of grief and silence. The once bustling caves, filled with the sound of scribes working to preserve the sacred texts, were now eerily quiet. The survivors moved like shadows, their eyes hollow, their hands trembling as they gathered what was left of their work.

Elijah had taken it upon himself to lead the efforts to recover and secure the remaining scrolls, though the task felt overwhelming in the wake of their losses. Ezra's death weighed heavily on him. The man who had been their guide and spiritual center was gone, and with him, it seemed, the clarity and focus that had once driven their mission. Now, every action felt burdened by doubt.

The raid had shaken them to the core, and though they had been able to hide some of the scrolls before the soldiers arrived, many were lost. The precious words of their ancestors, the scriptures they had devoted their lives to preserving, were scattered and burned, leaving only ashes in their place.

Elijah knelt in the corner of one of the caves, carefully unrolling a partially charred scroll. His hands shook as he read the words, some of them barely legible, the edges crumbling under his touch. The prophecy of Isaiah was still there, though the page was scarred, a painful reminder of what they had lost.

"By His wounds, we are healed."

The words felt like a whisper in the darkness, but Elijah clung to them, even as the rest of the world seemed to crumble around him. The prophecy had become more than just a message of hope—it had become his lifeline, the only thing tethering him to a future that still felt uncertain.

"Elijah." The voice was soft, hesitant.

He looked up to see Miriam standing at the entrance to the cave, her face pale but determined. Her wounds had begun to heal, though the physical pain was nothing compared to the emotional scars she carried. Since the raid, she had been distant, retreating into herself in a way that made Elijah ache with helplessness. She had always been the strong one, the voice of reason and hope. But now, that light seemed dimmed, and Elijah didn't know how to bring her back.

"We're gathering the survivors," Miriam said quietly, stepping further into the cave. "We need to talk about what comes next."

Elijah nodded, rising to his feet. He rolled the scroll carefully and placed it back among the others, his heart heavy with the knowledge that so much had been lost. But there was still something left, something worth fighting for. They couldn't give up now. Not when the prophecies still pointed toward the coming Messiah. Not when there was still hope, even if it was faint.

Together, they made their way to the main chamber, where the survivors had gathered. The group was smaller now, their faces etched with grief and fear. The air was thick with unspoken pain, the weight of their losses hanging over them like a storm cloud.

Abba Nathan's absence was painfully felt. Though he had survived the raid, the old man had retreated into solitude, spending his days in silent prayer and reflection. His faith remained unshaken, but his strength was waning. Elijah knew it was only a matter of time before the elder passed into the next life, leaving them to carry on the mission without his wisdom to guide them.

As the group settled, Elijah took a deep breath, his eyes scanning the room. "We've lost much," he began, his voice steady despite the turmoil within him.

"But we are not defeated. The scrolls that remain must be preserved. The Word must survive. That's why we're here. That's why Ezra gave his life."

The mention of Ezra's name sent a ripple of emotion through the group. Some nodded in agreement, while others stared at the ground, their faces drawn with exhaustion and doubt. Miriam stood beside him, her presence a quiet support, though Elijah could sense the conflict within her. She hadn't spoken much about her own feelings since the raid, but he knew she was struggling, just as he was.

One of the younger scribes, Benjamin, spoke up, his voice tight with frustration. "But what's the point?" he asked, his hands clenched into fists. "We've lost so many scrolls. We're hiding in these caves like rats while the soldiers destroy everything we care about. How can we keep fighting when everything is falling apart?"

Elijah's heart tightened at the question. He understood Benjamin's pain, his doubt. It was the same doubt that gnawed at Elijah's own soul, the same fear that whispered in his ear every time he opened a scroll and saw the scars of destruction. But he couldn't let that doubt take hold. Not now.

"We fight because we must," Elijah replied, his voice firm. "The scrolls that remain are still sacred. The Word is still alive. And as long as we have even one scroll, we have hope. The Messiah will come, and when He does, everything we've suffered will have meaning."

Benjamin shook his head, his expression hard. "But how can you be so sure, Elijah? How can you be so certain that the Messiah will come? Look at what's happening. People are dying. The scrolls are being destroyed. What if we're wrong?"

Elijah took a breath, steadying himself. He had asked himself the same question a hundred times since the raid, had doubted his own beliefs in the darkest moments of the night. But each time, he came back to the same truth—the truth of the prophecies.

"I'm not certain," Elijah admitted, his voice softer now. "But I have faith. I have faith that the suffering we endure now is part of something greater. The prophecies speak of the Messiah's coming, and I believe those words. Even if we can't see it yet, even if everything around us seems to be falling apart, the Messiah will come. And when He does, all of this—everything we've done, everything we've sacrificed—will have been worth it."

A heavy silence followed his words. The group sat in quiet contemplation, each person wrestling with their own doubts and fears. Elijah could see the weariness in their eyes, the weight of survival pressing down on them. But there was something else too, something deeper—a flicker of hope, faint but real. It was enough to keep them going. For now, it was enough.

That night, Elijah returned to his small chamber, his mind heavy with the weight of the day's discussion. He had spoken of hope, of faith, but the truth was, he still felt lost. Ezra's death had left a void that Elijah wasn't sure he could fill. The elder had been the guiding force behind their mission, the one who had kept them all focused on the greater purpose. Now, with him gone, it felt as though they were drifting, untethered and vulnerable.

As he sat in the quiet of his chamber, the faint sound of footsteps caught his attention. He looked up to see Jonas standing in the doorway, his face pale and lined with guilt. Elijah's chest tightened at the sight of him. Since the raid, Jonas had been a ghost, avoiding the group, staying on the outskirts of the caves. He hadn't spoken much, but Elijah knew the weight of his betrayal hung heavy on him.

"Elijah," Jonas said quietly, his voice trembling. "Can I speak with you?"

Elijah studied him for a moment, his emotions tangled. He still hadn't forgiven Jonas for what he had done, for the role he had played in leading the soldiers to Qumran. But he couldn't ignore the pain in Jonas' eyes, the way his hands shook as he stood in the doorway, barely able to meet Elijah's gaze.

"Come in," Elijah said, his voice neutral.

Jonas stepped into the chamber, his movements hesitant. He looked thinner, more gaunt, as though the guilt he carried had eaten away at him from the inside. He stood before Elijah, his head bowed, his hands clasped tightly together.

"I don't know how to say this," Jonas began, his voice shaking. "But I need to try. I'm sorry, Elijah. I'm so sorry for what I did. I didn't mean for any of this to happen. I thought I could protect you, protect all of us. But I was wrong. And now... now everything is ruined because of me."

Elijah felt a knot tighten in his chest. He wanted to be angry, wanted to lash out at Jonas for the pain he had caused. But all he could see now was a broken man, consumed by guilt and regret. The anger that had once burned so brightly within him had dimmed, replaced by something else—something closer to pity.

"What do you want me to say, Jonas?" Elijah asked, his voice soft. "That everything is forgiven? That we can go back to how things were?"

Jonas' head dropped lower, his shoulders sagging under the weight of his shame. "I don't expect forgiveness. I don't deserve it. But I need to make things right. I need to find a way to fix what I've broken."

Elijah studied him for a long moment, the silence between them heavy with unspoken pain. He could see the sincerity in Jonas' eyes, the desperation to atone for his actions. But trust was something that couldn't be rebuilt overnight, especially not after such a betrayal.

"You can't fix this, Jonas," Elijah said quietly. "Ezra is dead. The scrolls are destroyed. No amount of repentance will change that."

Jonas flinched, the truth of Elijah's words striking him like a blow. His eyes filled with tears, but he nodded, accepting the harsh reality.

"I know," Jonas whispered. "But I still have to try."

Elijah didn't respond immediately. He could see the torment in Jonas, the way the man was crumbling under the weight of his own guilt. Part of Elijah wanted to forgive him, to ease his burden. But another part of him—perhaps the stronger part—couldn't let go of the betrayal.

"Then do what you need to do," Elijah said, his voice distant. "But don't expect anything from me."

Jonas nodded, his face pale, his eyes filled with sorrow. Without another word, he turned and left the chamber, his footsteps echoing through the cave as he disappeared into the darkness.

Elijah sat in the silence that followed, his heart heavy. He wanted to believe that Jonas could be redeemed, that there was a way forward for all of them. But the losses they had suffered—the destruction, the deaths—they weren't so easily erased.

And yet, as Elijah sat alone in the darkness, the words of Isaiah 53 echoed in his mind once more, a quiet reminder of the suffering servant, of a redemption that would come through pain.

"By His wounds, we are healed."

Elijah closed his eyes, the weight of those words pressing down on him like a burden he wasn't sure he was strong enough to carry. But he would carry it, for as long as he had to. Because the Messiah was coming. And when He did, all of this—all the suffering, all the loss—would finally make sense.

Elijah sat in the cave long after Jonas had left, the weight of everything pressing down on him like the stones that surrounded him. The silence was thick, broken only by the distant sound of wind sweeping through the desert. He stared at the scrolls before him, the ones that had survived the raid, but their presence felt hollow in the face of all they had lost.

For the first time in his life, Elijah didn't know if he could carry on. The burden of preserving the Word, of protecting the prophecy, was too heavy. He had spoken of hope, of faith in the Messiah's coming, but deep down, he felt empty. The fire that had once driven him was flickering, the light dimming in the face of so much destruction.

He closed his eyes, trying to center himself, trying to grasp onto any piece of the faith that had sustained him. Isaiah 53 swirled in his mind, the words haunting him: "He was despised and rejected by men, a man of sorrows, and familiar with suffering." Each time he read it, he felt closer to the prophecy, but the closeness scared him. He saw himself in those words—suffering, broken, burdened by the sins of the world. The suffering servant had become not just a figure of future redemption, but a mirror of his own soul.

"Elijah."

Miriam's voice broke through the silence, soft and tentative. He opened his eyes to see her standing in the entrance, her body still weak from the injuries she had sustained in the raid. She had a way of moving now, cautious and deliberate, as though every step reminded her of the fragility of life. Her eyes were tired, but they still held a spark, that trace of defiance that had always been there, no matter what they had endured.

"I thought you might be here," she said, walking slowly toward him. She sat down beside him, the warmth of her presence a quiet comfort.

Elijah looked at her, his voice barely above a whisper. "I don't know if I can do this anymore."

Miriam didn't answer right away. She leaned her back against the stone wall, letting out a breath as though she had been holding it in for hours. She, too, carried the weight of loss, the pain of watching people she loved die and seeing their work destroyed. But even through all of it, Miriam had always been strong. It was her strength that had anchored Elijah more times than he could count.

"I understand," she said softly, her voice steady despite the sorrow that laced it. "But we don't have a choice, do we? If we stop now, everything we've worked for, everything we've sacrificed, will be for nothing."

Elijah's chest tightened. He knew she was right. They couldn't stop. The Messiah was coming, and the Word had to survive. But the words felt like an echo in his mind, distant and hollow.

"How do you do it?" he asked, turning to her. "How do you still believe, after everything?"

Miriam sighed, her gaze distant. "I don't know. Maybe I don't believe as much as I used to. But I know this much: we're still alive. We've survived, even when everything around us has been destroyed. There has to be a reason for that. There has to be something more than just suffering."

Elijah swallowed hard. He wanted to believe that there was something more, but after all they had been through, it was hard to hold onto that hope. The suffering servant, the prophecies—they felt so far removed from their current reality, from the destruction and death that seemed to follow them wherever they went.

"Do you think the Messiah will really come?" Elijah asked, his voice laced with doubt.

Miriam looked at him, her expression soft but firm. "I don't know. But I think we have to believe He will. If we give up on that... then what are we fighting for?"

Her words struck Elijah deeply. He had been so consumed by the prophecy of the suffering servant, so focused on the Messiah's coming, that he had forgotten why they had started this mission in the first place. They weren't just preserving words on parchment—they were preserving hope. The hope that the Messiah would come, that their people would be redeemed, that their suffering would not be in vain.

Elijah closed his eyes, taking a deep breath. Miriam was right. He had to keep going, not just for the prophecy, but for the people who had died, for the ones who had sacrificed everything for the Word. For Ezra.

He opened his eyes, his gaze steady. "You're right. We have to believe. We have to keep going."

Miriam nodded, her expression softening. "We'll make it through this, Elijah. We always do."

The following morning, the survivors of Qumran gathered in the main chamber once more. There were fewer of them now, their faces etched with grief and exhaustion, but the weight of their purpose still hung in the air. Despite everything, the Word remained. And that was enough to keep them moving forward.

Elijah stood before the group, his heart heavy with the responsibility of leadership that had been thrust upon him. He wasn't sure he was ready for this, wasn't sure he could fill the void that Ezra had left behind. But as he looked at the faces of those who remained—the scribes, the scholars, the faithful who had risked everything for the Word—he knew he had no choice.

"We've lost much," Elijah began, his voice steady despite the turmoil within him. "But we are still here. And as long as we are here, the Word lives. The scrolls that remain must be preserved. We cannot allow the suffering we've endured to be for nothing."

The group listened in silence, their eyes heavy with the weight of his words.

"The prophecy of Isaiah 53 speaks of suffering," Elijah continued, "but it also speaks of redemption. The Messiah will come, even if we cannot yet see it. Our mission is to prepare the way for Him. That is why we are here."

There was a murmur of agreement, though it was tinged with doubt. The raid had shaken them, had made them question everything. But Elijah knew that if they gave up now, if they let go of the hope that had sustained them, all would be lost.

"We will rebuild," Elijah said firmly, his voice rising. "We will continue our work. And when the Messiah comes, He will find the Word intact, because we did not give up."

The group nodded, though their faces were still marked by grief. But there was a flicker of hope in their eyes, a small but steady light that reminded Elijah of why they had come here in the first place.

In the days that followed, the survivors began to recover what remained of the scrolls. It was a painstaking process, one that took time and patience, but it was also a reminder of the resilience of their mission. The Word had not been completely destroyed. Some of the texts had survived the raid, and those that were lost could be rewritten, transcribed from memory by the scholars who had dedicated their lives to preserving them.

Elijah threw himself into the work, his hands once again stained with ink as he copied the sacred texts. The process brought a sense of purpose, a quiet focus that helped ease the pain of loss. Each word he copied felt like a small act of defiance against the darkness that had threatened to consume them.

Miriam, too, found solace in the work. Though her injuries still pained her, she refused to remain idle. She helped where she could, working alongside Elijah and the others, her presence a quiet but steady force. Her wounds, both physical and emotional, were still healing, but she never spoke of her pain. Instead, she pressed on, determined to see their mission through to the end.

It was in the quiet moments between them that Elijah began to see the depth of her strength. She had always been resilient, always been the one to keep him grounded. But now, after everything they had endured, he realized just how much he relied on her, how much her presence gave him the strength to carry on.

One evening, as the last light of day faded from the sky, Elijah and Miriam sat together near the entrance of the cave. The air was cool, the wind gentle as it swept across the desert. The stars above were faint, barely visible against the deepening darkness.

For a long time, neither of them spoke. The silence between them was comfortable, a shared understanding that didn't require words.

"I've been thinking," Miriam said softly, breaking the quiet.

Elijah turned to her, his expression curious. "About what?"

"About everything that's happened," she replied, her gaze fixed on the horizon. "The suffering, the losses... it's easy to get lost in it, to let the grief consume us."

Elijah nodded, though he didn't speak. He knew exactly what she meant.

"But I think," Miriam continued, her voice steady, "that the suffering isn't the end. It's part of the journey, part of what we have to go through to reach redemption."

Elijah frowned, her words stirring something within him. "You're talking about the suffering servant."

Miriam nodded, her eyes soft. "Yes. I think that's what the prophecy means. The suffering we're enduring now—it's not pointless. It's leading us somewhere. To something greater."

Elijah's chest tightened. He had thought the same, had clung to the prophecy as a way to make sense of the pain. But hearing Miriam speak of it with such conviction made it feel more real, more tangible.

"Do you think... do you think we'll see the Messiah?" Elijah asked quietly.

Miriam was silent for a moment, her gaze thoughtful. "I don't know," she admitted. "But I believe we're preparing the way for Him. And if we don't see Him, others will. That's why this matters. That's why we can't give up."

Elijah looked at her, his heart swelling with a mixture of hope and sorrow. She had always been the stronger one, always the one to see the light when everything else seemed dark. And now, even after everything they had lost, she still believed in the future they were working toward.

"We won't give up," Elijah said softly, his voice filled with quiet resolve. "We'll keep fighting. For the Messiah. For the Word. For each other."

Miriam smiled, a small but genuine smile that lit up the darkness around them. "For each other," she echoed.

And in that moment, Elijah knew that no matter what happened next, no matter what trials lay ahead, they would face them together.

Chapter 7: The Maccabean Uprising

The sound of swords clashing, the heavy thud of shields, and the battle cries of men echoed through the valleys, reverberating in Elijah's chest like the pounding of his own heart. The Maccabean revolt was in full force, and everywhere, the air was thick with the scent of rebellion. From the hills of Judea to the hidden caves of Qumran, the Jewish people had risen against Antiochus IV Epiphanes and his oppressive regime. There was a fire in the hearts of men now—a hope for freedom, for redemption, and the restoration of their temple.

In the heart of Qumran, Elijah paced near the entrance of the caves, his hands stained with ink, his mind a battleground of its own. The Maccabees were fighting with everything they had, and each day, the call to arms grew louder in his ears. He wanted to join them. He wanted to fight alongside Judas Maccabeus and the Jewish forces who were pushing back against the Seleucids. The urge for justice burned within him—justice for Ezra, for the slain scribes, for the desecrated scrolls. But another force, quieter but just as insistent, pulled him in the opposite direction: the prophecy.

Elijah had read it countless times. Isaiah 53 spoke of a suffering servant, of redemption through pain and sacrifice. The scrolls that remained in Qumran were fragile, sacred pieces of history that he and the others had risked everything to preserve. Their work was not yet done. The Messiah had not yet come. How could he abandon that?

"Elijah."

Miriam's voice broke through his thoughts, her presence beside him a steady, comforting force. She had been watching him, sensing the inner turmoil that had taken root in his soul. Miriam had always been able to read him, even when he could not understand himself.

"They need you," she said quietly, her eyes scanning the horizon where the battle raged in the distance.

Elijah clenched his fists, the tension coiling in his muscles. "I know. I can hear them. But... the scrolls, the prophecy. What if we leave and the work is never finished?"

Miriam turned to him, her face softened by understanding. "The work will never be finished, Elijah. Not like that. The scrolls will survive, as they always have. But what we are fighting for—freedom, redemption—those are also part of the prophecy. Don't you see? It's all connected."

He shook his head, frustration tightening his chest. "How can I be sure? How can I know that what we're doing will lead to the Messiah? How can I—"

Miriam placed a hand on his arm, stilling his frantic thoughts. Her touch was gentle but firm, grounding him in the present. "Faith, Elijah. That's all we have. The prophecy will be fulfilled, but we cannot see the entire path. Sometimes, we have to take steps without knowing where they lead."

Her words sank into him like rain on dry soil, but they didn't ease the conflict inside. He looked toward the horizon, where the Maccabees fought for the soul of Israel. Judas Maccabeus had already reclaimed parts of Jerusalem, and the Seleucids were on the defensive, but the battle was far from over. If Elijah stayed here in Qumran, was he abandoning his people? Was he abandoning justice?

"I'm afraid," he admitted, his voice barely a whisper.

Miriam's gaze softened. "We all are. But that doesn't mean we should run from the fight. You can still be part of this, Elijah. Even if you're here, you can help the revolt."

"How?" he asked, his voice thick with emotion. "By hiding in caves, transcribing ancient scrolls while others fight and die?"

Miriam smiled faintly, her eyes gleaming with that quiet determination that had always drawn him to her. "You've done more than that. You've preserved the Word. You've kept the faith alive when everything else was falling apart. And now, we can support the Maccabees in other ways. We can offer shelter, supplies, and, most importantly, hope."

Elijah looked at her, a knot tightening in his throat. She was right, as she so often was. They were not warriors, not soldiers in the way the Maccabees were. But they could still fight, in their own way. And perhaps, just perhaps, that was what the prophecy required of him.

The next morning, the camp buzzed with the news of another battle. Judas Maccabeus had led his forces into a critical skirmish against Antiochus' army, pushing them back toward the hills. The revolt was gaining momentum, and with it, hope spread like wildfire among the people.

But with the news came something darker—rumors of a Seleucid plot, a secret plan to launch a devastating attack on the Maccabean forces. It would be a strike designed to crush the rebellion before it could gain any more ground. If the Maccabees weren't warned, if they didn't act quickly, the rebellion would fall.

Jonas, who had been staying on the outskirts of the camp, away from the others, heard the whispers of the soldiers moving in the night. His heart pounded as he listened, piecing together fragments of conversation. The attack was planned for dawn. They would strike the Maccabean forces while they were vulnerable, wiping out the core of the rebellion in a single blow.

Jonas stood frozen in the shadows, his mind racing. He had been a part of this once—this machine of betrayal and violence. But now, things were different. Now, he understood the cost. His betrayal had already led to the deaths of so many. He had seen the destruction of Qumran, had seen the pain in Elijah's eyes, the loss in Miriam's. He had carried that weight with him, every step of his journey since the raid. But this—this was his chance to make things right.

Without thinking, Jonas slipped away from the camp, moving quickly toward the hills where the Maccabees were gathered. The air was cold, the desert silent except for the soft rustle of his footsteps. He knew the way. He had memorized the paths through the hills, the places where soldiers and spies lingered in the dark.

This was his last chance. His last chance to atone for what he had done.

Elijah stood outside the caves, his heart heavy with indecision. He had spent the morning going over the scrolls, trying to find solace in the words of the prophets. But no matter how many times he read the passages, his thoughts kept returning to the revolt, to the battle that raged not far from where they stood.

Miriam had gone into the camp earlier, bringing supplies and information to the Maccabees. She believed in the revolt, in the fight for freedom, and though she had never said it outright, Elijah could sense that she wanted him to believe in it too.

But he was still torn.

What was his role in all of this? Was he meant to stay here, in Qumran, and preserve the Word, or was he meant to join the fight, to take up arms alongside Judas and the others?

As the sun climbed higher into the sky, Elijah's thoughts were interrupted by the sound of frantic footsteps approaching. He turned to see one of the younger scribes running toward him, breathless and wide-eyed.

"Elijah!" the young man called out, his voice strained. "It's Jonas... he's gone!"

Elijah frowned, confusion rippling through him. "Gone? What do you mean?"

"He left this morning," the scribe explained, his words tumbling over each other. "We don't know where, but he took a horse and rode toward the Maccabean camp. He didn't tell anyone where he was going, but... but I think he's trying to warn them."

Elijah's chest tightened. Jonas. The man who had betrayed them, the man who had brought the soldiers to Qumran and caused the deaths of so many. He had been distant since the raid, consumed by guilt, but Elijah had never expected this.

"Warn them about what?" Elijah asked, though a sinking feeling had already begun to settle in his stomach.

The scribe looked at him, fear in his eyes. "There's a plot. A plan to attack the Maccabees at dawn. Jonas must have found out."

Elijah's heart pounded in his chest. If Jonas was right, if the Maccabees were walking into a trap, they had to act quickly. But Jonas was on his own, and if the attack was already in motion...

Without another word, Elijah turned and began running toward the hills. The wind whipped at his cloak, the sand kicking up beneath his feet as he raced through the narrow passages that led to the Maccabean camp. His mind was a blur of thoughts, of fear and hope and desperation.

Jonas. After everything he had done, after all the pain and destruction he had caused, was this how he would seek redemption? Was this his way of atoning for the betrayal that had shattered their world?

Elijah didn't know. But he had to find out.

By the time Elijah reached the Maccabean camp, the sun was beginning to set, casting long shadows across the hills. The camp was alive with activity—soldiers preparing for the next battle, messengers running back and forth, their faces tight with determination. But there was an undercurrent of fear, a tension that crackled in the air.

"Elijah!"

Miriam's voice cut through the noise, and Elijah turned to see her hurrying toward him, her face pale with worry. She had heard the news, had seen the look of panic on his face as he arrived.

"What's happening?" she asked, her voice tight with urgency. "What did you hear?"

Elijah took a deep breath, trying to steady himself. "Jonas. He's gone to warn the Maccabees. There's a plan to attack them at dawn, a trap set by Antiochus' forces. He went alone."

Miriam's eyes widened, shock rippling across her face. "Jonas? He... he's trying to warn them?"

Elijah nodded, the weight of the situation pressing down on him. "I don't know if he'll make it in time. But we have to try."

The hours that followed were a blur of preparation and fear. The Maccabees, now warned of the impending attack, began to mobilize their forces, setting up defensive positions in the hills. Elijah and Miriam watched from a distance, their hearts heavy with uncertainty.

And then, as the first light of dawn began to creep over the horizon, the sound of battle erupted.

The Seleucid forces, unaware that their plan had been discovered, charged into the valley, their war cries filling the air. But the Maccabees were ready. The trap that had been set for them had been turned against the enemy, and the Jewish forces struck back with a fury that had been building for years.

Elijah stood on a ridge, watching as the battle unfolded below. His heart pounded in his chest, fear and hope warring within him. He had no idea where Jonas was, or if he had survived long enough to deliver the warning. But as he watched the tide of battle shift, he knew that the Maccabees had been given a fighting chance.

The battle raged for hours, the sound of steel against steel echoing through the hills. Elijah's breath caught in his throat as he saw the Seleucid forces begin to retreat, their once formidable army now broken and scattered.

Victory. The Maccabees had won.

It wasn't until after the battle had ended, when the sun was high in the sky and the air was thick with the scent of blood and dust, that Elijah found Jonas.

He was lying near the edge of the battlefield, his body broken and battered. Blood stained the ground around him, and his breaths came in shallow, ragged gasps. Elijah knelt beside him, his heart heavy with a mixture of grief and gratitude.

"Jonas," Elijah whispered, his voice thick with emotion.

Jonas' eyes fluttered open, his gaze hazy but focused on Elijah. A faint smile tugged at his lips. "I did it," he rasped, his voice barely audible. "I... I warned them."

Elijah's chest tightened, tears burning in his eyes. "You did. You saved them."

Jonas coughed, a wet, painful sound. "I had to. I had to make things right."

Elijah nodded, his hand gripping Jonas' as the man's life slipped away. "You did."

Jonas' eyes closed, his body stilling as the last breath left his lips. For a long moment, Elijah sat there, holding the hand of the man who had once been their betrayer, the man who had now given his life for their redemption.

It was in that moment that Elijah realized the truth of the prophecy, the truth that had eluded him for so long. Redemption was not about perfection. It was not about being without flaw. It was about sacrifice, about giving everything, even when you had nothing left to give.

Jonas had been the suffering servant in his own way, and through his death, he had helped pave the way for something greater.

Elijah sat beside Jonas's lifeless body, the weight of the moment sinking into him like stones dropped into a deep well. The battle was over, the Maccabees victorious, but there was no joy in his heart—only the somber reality of what they had lost. Jonas, the man who had betrayed them, had found a form of redemption, but the cost had been his life.

As the chaos of the battlefield faded into the distance, the sense of victory was tempered by the sight of those who had fallen. The bodies of the slain littered the hillsides, men who had fought for their people, their land, and their God. Elijah's chest ached with the enormity of it all. He had spoken of hope, of faith in the prophecy, but seeing the cost in human lives shook him to his core.

Jonas's final words echoed in his mind: "I had to make things right." He had, in his own way. But what had it all meant? Was this redemption? Was this what the prophecy had foretold—a man's final act of sacrifice to save others? Elijah couldn't help but wonder how it all fit together. Jonas's death had saved the Maccabees from a catastrophic defeat, but Elijah's mind drifted back to the larger battle that loomed, the spiritual war still to be fought.

"Elijah."

Miriam's voice pulled him from his thoughts. She stood behind him, her face pale but resolute. Her gaze fell on Jonas, and a shadow of sadness passed over her features. "He did it, didn't he?"

Elijah nodded, his throat tight. "He warned them. Without him, the attack would have been a disaster. The Maccabees would have been destroyed."

Miriam knelt beside him, her hand resting on his arm. "He found a way to redeem himself."

Elijah didn't respond immediately, his eyes fixed on Jonas's still form. The redemption Jonas had sought was a reflection of the prophecy that had been haunting Elijah for weeks—the suffering servant, the one who would bear the weight of others' sins and bring salvation through sacrifice. But was this the kind of redemption that the prophecy foretold? Was this what it meant to prepare the way for the Messiah?

"He gave his life for them," Elijah said finally, his voice heavy. "For us. After everything he had done... he still found a way to make it right."

Miriam's eyes softened, her expression filled with quiet sorrow. "It's never too late for redemption, Elijah. The prophecy teaches us that much."

Elijah nodded, though his heart was still tangled with the complexity of it all. He had believed in the prophecy, had clung to it when everything else had fallen apart. But now, seeing Jonas's sacrifice, he began to understand its deeper meaning. Redemption wasn't a single moment. It wasn't just about a Messiah coming to save them—it was about the choices they made, the sacrifices they offered in the face of insurmountable odds.

Miriam squeezed his arm gently. "Come. We need to help the others."

As they moved through the camp, helping the wounded and gathering what remained of the supplies, Elijah's thoughts continued to swirl around the events of the day. The Maccabees had won a crucial victory, one that would strengthen their resolve and inspire hope across Judea. The revolt against Antiochus was gaining momentum, and the dream of a free Israel seemed closer than ever.

But for Elijah, the physical victory was only part of the story. The battle may have been won, but his heart was still restless. The work they had begun in Qumran—the preservation of the scrolls, the sacred words of the prophets—remained unfinished. The rebellion was a fight for the present, for the restoration of their people and their land, but Elijah's mind was on something larger, something that transcended the immediate.

He found himself standing at the edge of the camp, gazing out at the hills that led back to Qumran. His mind drifted to the scrolls, the prophecies, the words that had been entrusted to them. Was that where his true calling lay? Was his role in this uprising not to fight with swords, but with the preservation of the Word, ensuring that future generations would know the truth of the prophecies?

Miriam approached him, her face weary but determined. "You're thinking about Qumran, aren't you?"

Elijah didn't answer right away. He had been struggling with this question for days—torn between his desire to join the fight and his responsibility to the mission they had started. "I don't know what I'm supposed to do," he admitted, his voice quiet.

Miriam stepped beside him, her eyes scanning the distant hills. "We're all fighting in our own way, Elijah. You don't have to pick up a sword to be part of this."

"But what if I should be doing more?" Elijah's voice cracked with the weight of his inner conflict. "What if preserving the Word isn't enough? What if we never see the Messiah? What if we're doing all this for nothing?"

Miriam looked at him, her eyes filled with a deep understanding. "I don't believe that for a second. We may not see the Messiah in our lifetime, but that doesn't mean our work is in vain. Everything we do here—preserving the scrolls, supporting the revolt—leads toward something greater. We're part of the story, Elijah, but we're not the whole story."

Elijah's chest tightened at her words. She was right, as she so often was. He had been so focused on the immediate, on the fight in front of him, that he had forgotten the larger picture. The prophecy was not just about their present struggle—it was about the future, about preparing the way for the Messiah, even if they never saw the fulfillment of that promise in their lifetime.

"Jonas found redemption in the end," Miriam continued, her voice soft. "And so will we. We just have to keep going."

Elijah closed his eyes, the truth of her words sinking in. Jonas's death had shown him something he hadn't been able to see before—redemption wasn't a single, glorious moment. It was a path, a series of choices, a journey. And they were all on that journey, together.

The camp was buzzing with the aftermath of the battle, and the Maccabean forces were celebrating their hard-won victory. But Elijah and Miriam knew that the fight was far from over. Antiochus's forces would regroup, and more battles would follow. The road ahead was long and treacherous, but for the first time in weeks, Elijah felt a renewed sense of purpose.

The next morning, Elijah stood with Judas Maccabeus and the other leaders of the revolt as they discussed their plans. Judas was a formidable leader, his presence commanding respect from all who stood in his circle. His eyes, sharp and intense, scanned the faces of his men as he spoke of strategy and the next steps in their fight for freedom.

"Elijah," Judas said, turning to him, "you've done much for us already, but I must ask—will you stay with us? We need men like you, men of faith, to help lead our people."

Elijah hesitated, the weight of Judas's words pressing down on him. The desire to fight alongside these men, to be part of this historic uprising, was strong. But in his heart, he knew where he was needed.

"I'm honored, Judas," Elijah said, his voice steady. "But my place is in Qumran. There are scrolls there, sacred texts that must be preserved. The Word is as important as this battle, and I cannot abandon that mission."

Judas regarded him for a moment, his eyes thoughtful. "I understand," he said finally, his voice filled with respect. "The Word is the foundation of our people. Without it, we are nothing. Go, and may God be with you."

Elijah nodded, feeling the tension ease from his chest. He had made his choice. The path before him was clear now, even if the road was difficult. He would return to Qumran, continue the work of preserving the Word, and prepare the way for the Messiah.

As Elijah and Miriam prepared to leave the Maccabean camp, a quiet sense of resolution settled over them. They had fought in their own way, had contributed to the victory of the revolt, but their journey was not over.

Before they left, Elijah knelt beside Jonas's grave, his heart heavy with both grief and gratitude. He hadn't forgiven Jonas for everything, not fully, but in the end, the man had found a way to redeem himself. And that, Elijah realized, was part of the prophecy too.

"By His wounds, we are healed," Elijah whispered, the words of Isaiah 53 rising in his mind. He closed his eyes, feeling the truth of those words deep in his soul. The prophecy of the suffering servant wasn't just about one man—it was about all of them. It was about the path of redemption, about the choices they made, the sacrifices they offered. And even in betrayal, there was the possibility of redemption.

The journey back to Qumran was quiet, the wind sweeping across the barren landscape as Elijah and Miriam walked side by side. The scrolls awaited them, the sacred texts that held the words of the prophets, the hope of their people. The victory of the Maccabees had restored something in Elijah—an understanding that their mission was far larger than a single battle, far larger than any one of them.

Miriam looked at him, her face calm but filled with the quiet strength that had always grounded him. "We're doing the right thing, Elijah. The Messiah will come. And when He does, the Word will be ready."

Elijah nodded, his heart swelling with a renewed sense of hope. "Yes," he said softly. "The Messiah will come."

The return to Qumran was a journey marked by silence. The desert stretched endlessly before Elijah and Miriam, its vastness a reflection of the uncertainties that weighed on their hearts. Every step carried them further from the bloodied fields of battle, and yet Elijah couldn't shake the feeling that the war was not behind him. Though he had chosen not to fight with swords, he was still very much in the midst of a different kind of battle—a spiritual one, where the stakes were not merely land or freedom, but the soul of a people.

Miriam walked beside him, her face etched with a quiet strength that had become her hallmark. She had grown since the days before the raid on

Qumran, and though the physical wounds from that attack had largely healed, the scars beneath the surface remained. Her faith, however, had not wavered. If anything, it had deepened, and Elijah found himself drawing strength from her resolve.

The wind kicked up dust around their feet as they approached the familiar caves. Qumran stood before them like a sentinel in the wilderness, its stone walls bathed in the fading light of the afternoon sun. Elijah's heart beat a little faster as the entrance came into view. He had left Qumran torn between his desire for immediate justice and his commitment to the long road of preserving the Word. Now, having returned from the Maccabean camp, he felt a sense of clarity he hadn't had before.

Yet even as they neared the safety of the caves, the memory of Jonas's sacrifice weighed heavily on his mind. The image of Jonas lying lifeless on the battlefield still haunted him. Elijah knew that Jonas had sought redemption in his final moments, and though he had died to save others, the tragedy of his betrayal still lingered like a shadow over his sacrifice.

"He gave everything to warn them," Miriam said quietly, as if reading Elijah's thoughts.

Elijah nodded. "But I wonder if it was enough."

Miriam turned to him, her expression serious. "It was enough. Jonas did what he could, even if it came at the very end. Redemption isn't about living a perfect life, Elijah. It's about turning back when everything is telling you to keep going in the wrong direction. Jonas found that path, even if it was too late to undo the damage."

Her words, gentle but firm, echoed the truth that Elijah had been grappling with since they'd left the battlefield. Redemption was not something earned by perfect choices but by sacrifice. Jonas had given his life for the Maccabees, and that, in the end, had to count for something. Still, Elijah couldn't help but feel that their battle wasn't just about lives lost and saved—it was about the future they were trying to build. The spiritual victory, the one the prophets had spoken of, still lay ahead.

As they reached the entrance of the caves, the scribes and scholars who had remained in Qumran greeted them. The faces that welcomed Elijah and Miriam back were a mixture of relief and quiet anticipation. Word of the Maccabean victories had spread, and though Qumran was isolated from the main conflict, they all knew that the tide of war was shifting. Freedom was within reach, and with it, the possibility of returning to a life where their work could continue without fear of destruction.

Abba Nathan, now frail and moving slowly, was among those who greeted them. His wise eyes met Elijah's, and in that gaze, Elijah saw something that steadied him—a reminder that their mission was far from over. Nathan had always been the spiritual anchor of Qumran, and though age had slowed his movements, his faith had not dimmed.

"You've returned at a critical time," Abba Nathan said, his voice a low murmur as he clasped Elijah's arm. "There is much work to be done. The scrolls are waiting, and so are the people."

Elijah felt the weight of those words settle on his shoulders. "We've seen much," he said softly. "Jonas... he gave his life to save the Maccabees. But now, the fight for the future continues."

Nathan's eyes softened with understanding. "Sacrifice always leaves its mark, Elijah. But you've come back with something more than just a story of battle. You've come back with the knowledge that redemption doesn't end in one man's sacrifice. It continues, generation after generation."

Over the next several days, the rhythm of life in Qumran began to settle once again. The scribes resumed their work, carefully transcribing the sacred texts, their hands moving with precision over the worn parchment. The raid had destroyed many of their scrolls, but there were still enough left to continue the mission. Each word they copied felt like an act of defiance against the forces that sought to erase their history.

Elijah threw himself into the work with renewed focus, yet his thoughts often wandered to the broader conflict beyond the walls of Qumran. The Maccabees were still fighting, and though they had won a crucial victory, the war was not yet over. Antiochus would not give up easily. There would be more battles, more bloodshed before the land was free.

Miriam, too, had become more involved in the work of Qumran, though her heart still pulled her toward the fight for freedom. She had spent hours speaking with the survivors, encouraging them and sharing news from the front lines. She had become a quiet leader among them, her words offering hope in a time when it was most needed.

One evening, as the last light of the sun disappeared behind the hills, Miriam approached Elijah. He had been working late, his hands stained with ink as he carefully copied a scroll of Isaiah. The prophecy of the suffering servant had once again consumed his thoughts, and he found himself reading and rereading the passages, searching for answers.

"Elijah," Miriam said softly, sitting beside him, "you've been distant since we returned."

He looked up at her, surprised by her gentle accusation. "I've been working," he said simply. "There's so much to do. The scrolls..."

Miriam shook her head. "It's not just the scrolls. You've been carrying something with you since the battle. You haven't let it go."

Elijah sighed, setting the scroll aside. He knew she was right, but he wasn't sure how to explain the storm inside him. "I've been thinking about Jonas," he admitted, his voice low. "About his sacrifice. I know he found redemption in the end, but I can't shake the feeling that his death is a symbol of something more."

Miriam tilted her head, her eyes thoughtful. "What do you mean?"

Elijah hesitated, choosing his words carefully. "Jonas's death wasn't just about saving the Maccabees. It was about showing us that even in the darkest moments, redemption is possible. It's the same with the prophecy of Isaiah 53. The suffering servant... I think I understand it better now. It's not just about one man suffering for the sins of many. It's about all of us. It's about the way we carry the weight of our own mistakes, how we choose to sacrifice ourselves for others."

Miriam's eyes softened, a small smile tugging at her lips. "You're seeing it clearly now, Elijah. The prophecy isn't just about the future—it's about the present. We're living it, every day."

Elijah felt a swell of emotion rise in his chest. For so long, he had been focused on the coming of the Messiah, on the idea that redemption would only arrive when the prophecy was fulfilled. But now, after everything he had seen, after Jonas's death and the victories of the Maccabees, he realized that redemption was already unfolding. It was in the choices they made, the sacrifices they offered, the way they continued to fight for the future, even when the odds were against them.

"It's hard to keep hoping," Elijah admitted, his voice barely above a whisper. "Especially when the suffering feels endless."

Miriam reached for his hand, her touch warm and reassuring. "Hope isn't about certainty, Elijah. It's about believing in something greater, even when you can't see the whole picture. That's what the prophecy teaches us. The Messiah will come, but our redemption doesn't have to wait for Him. It's already happening, right here."

Elijah looked at her, a new sense of clarity settling over him. Miriam was right. The prophecy wasn't something distant, something that would only be fulfilled in the future. It was happening now, in their lives, in their choices, in the sacrifices they made for each other.

In the days that followed, Elijah felt a renewed sense of purpose. His work in Qumran took on new meaning, not just as a way to preserve the scrolls but as a way to live out the prophecy he had come to understand so deeply. The battles being fought by the Maccabees were crucial, but so too was the work they were doing in the caves. Together, these efforts would pave the way for the Messiah, even if they never saw Him with their own eyes.

Abba Nathan, though weaker by the day, continued to guide them with his wisdom. He often spoke of the Daniel 8:14 prophecy, reminding them that the temple would be cleansed after a period of suffering. The physical victories of the Maccabees were a sign of that, but Elijah began to see that the real cleansing, the real redemption, would come from something deeper—from the spiritual renewal of their people.

One afternoon, as Elijah and Miriam stood at the entrance of the caves, watching the distant horizon, she turned to him, her expression thoughtful. "Do you think we'll see it?" she asked quietly.

"See what?" Elijah replied, though he already knew what she meant.

"The Messiah. Do you think we'll live to see Him come?"

Elijah smiled softly, the question no longer filled him with uncertainty. "I don't know," he said honestly. "But I think that's not the point. Whether we see Him or not, we're preparing the way. That's what matters."

Miriam nodded, her face softening with understanding. "We're part of the story."

Elijah's gaze drifted to the hills, where the sun was beginning to set, casting a golden light over the desert. "Yes," he said quietly. "We're part of the story. And that's enough."

Chapter 8: The Birth of Hope

The air of Jerusalem had changed. No longer did it carry the oppressive weight of Antiochus' cruelty. Instead, it was filled with the sound of life returning—children laughing, families rebuilding, priests once again lighting the sacred lamps in the newly purified temple. The revolt had succeeded. Judas Maccabeus and his forces had reclaimed the city, and the desecrated temple had been cleansed, just as the prophet Daniel had foretold.

Yet, despite the victory, Elijah felt a strange heaviness in his heart. The sight of the temple restored, its gates open once more to the faithful, should have filled him with joy, but he found himself restless, as if this triumph were only a small piece of a much larger puzzle. Even as the people rejoiced, Elijah's thoughts drifted back to the caves of Qumran, to the prophecies he had come to know so intimately. He had glimpsed the future in the ancient words of the prophets, and while the physical restoration of the temple was a victory, it wasn't the ultimate redemption they were waiting for.

It wasn't the Messiah.

As they returned to Qumran, the journey through the desert was quieter than before. The wind swept over the dunes, carrying with it a sense of expectation, but also weariness. The group of scribes, led by Elijah and Miriam, was smaller now, but there was a renewed determination among them. They had survived the horrors of Antiochus' reign, witnessed the cleansing of the temple, and now, they had come back to continue their work.

Elijah, however, could feel the strain of the journey in his bones. The victories had been hard-won, and while the group had returned to Qumran with hope, Elijah's body and spirit were exhausted. His hands were still steady as he transcribed the sacred scrolls, but the fire that once burned so fiercely in his chest now flickered weakly. He spent long hours in the scriptorium, hunched over the scrolls, but his mind often wandered.

He couldn't shake the dreams.

They had started soon after they left Jerusalem, vivid and intense, filling his sleep with images of a child—a child who would change the world. At first, Elijah dismissed them as the product of his exhaustion, but the dreams persisted, growing clearer each night. The child appeared in a humble setting, born not in a palace or a temple, but in a small village. A star hovered above, and the light that surrounded the child was unlike anything Elijah had ever seen.

Bethlehem. The name whispered through his mind each morning when he awoke, the image of the child lingering long after sleep had fled. The prophecy from Micah 5:2 played over and over in his head: "But you, Bethlehem Ephrathah, though you are small among the clans of Judah, out of you will come for me one who will be ruler over Israel, whose origins are from of old, from ancient times."

The words had always intrigued Elijah, but now they consumed him. His hands would tremble as he wrote them, feeling as though they held a secret he was just on the verge of uncovering. It was as if his life, his entire purpose, had become focused on this one prophecy, on the arrival of this child who would bring true redemption. He had to be ready. The world had to be ready.

Miriam watched him carefully during this time, her own body undergoing changes as well. She had felt it not long after they returned to Qumran—a faint fluttering within her, like a whisper of new life. It had been weeks since she had been certain, and now, as her belly swelled, the truth could no longer be denied. She was with child.

The news had spread quickly among the group, and there had been rejoicing. After so much death and destruction, the promise of new life was a balm to their weary souls. Miriam felt it too, though her joy was mingled with a deeper understanding of what this child represented. It wasn't just her own hope or Elijah's that she carried—this child was a symbol for their people, a new generation that would rise after the darkness of the revolt. It was a reminder that life continued, even in the midst of suffering, and that redemption was not a distant dream but something that could begin in the smallest, most humble places.

Miriam, though excited, was also concerned. She had seen the way Elijah had changed since the victory in Jerusalem. He had become more intense, more distant, his mind constantly turning over the prophecies, especially the one from Micah. The dreams he had shared with her filled her with a strange mix of awe and worry. He spoke of the child with a kind of fervor that sometimes made her wonder if he saw their own child as part of this divine plan.

"Elijah," she said one evening, sitting beside him as he worked late into the night. "You've hardly slept."

Elijah didn't look up from the scroll he was copying, his eyes focused on the delicate lines of text. "There's too much to do."

Miriam placed a gentle hand on his arm. "You can't do everything yourself. The others can help."

Elijah finally looked up, and she could see the weariness in his eyes, but also the fire that still burned there. "It's not just about copying the scrolls, Miriam. It's about preparing. Don't you see? The Messiah is coming. The prophecies are all pointing to it. And in my dreams... I see Him. A child, born in Bethlehem."

Miriam's heart ached at his intensity. She had always admired Elijah's devotion to the Word, but lately, his focus had become almost obsessive. "You can't know for sure when the Messiah will come," she said softly. "We may not live to see it."

Elijah shook his head, his voice low but fervent. "No. It's soon. I can feel it. The child in my dreams, He's real. He's the one. And we have to be ready."

Miriam studied him for a long moment, her own heart caught between hope and fear. She knew Elijah's visions were not just figments of his imagination—he had always had a deep connection to the prophecies, a kind of spiritual insight that set him apart. But she also knew that the strain of the past years had taken a toll on him, physically and emotionally.

"Elijah," she said gently, "you're exhausted. You've been carrying so much for so long. Let me help you."

Elijah reached out and took her hand, his fingers brushing over her palm in a rare moment of tenderness. "You are helping," he said, his voice softening. "You've always helped me. And now... with our child..." His voice trailed off, his eyes moving to her swelling belly, a look of wonder crossing his face.

Miriam smiled, though it was tinged with sadness. "Our child will be part of this story, Elijah. But we can't lose ourselves in the waiting. We have to live, too."

Elijah nodded slowly, his gaze distant. "I know. But it feels so close, Miriam. Closer than ever."

As the months passed, Miriam's pregnancy became a source of joy and hope for the community at Qumran. She took on a nurturing role, caring for those who had been wounded during the revolt and helping to rebuild the community after the destruction of the raid. Her presence brought a calmness to the group, a sense that, despite the hardships they had endured, life continued.

Abba Nathan, though growing weaker with age, had taken a special interest in Miriam's child. He often spoke to her about the prophecies, reminding her of Malachi's words about the messenger who would prepare the way for the Messiah. "Your child," he told her one day as they walked along the edge of the desert, "represents the future of our people. A new generation, born after so much suffering. This is how we rebuild. This is how we prepare."

Miriam had smiled at his words, though her thoughts often returned to Elijah and his obsession with the prophecy from Micah. Abba Nathan's wisdom brought comfort, but she could see how the strain was affecting Elijah. He had thrown himself deeper into the work, often losing himself in the scrolls for hours at a time, his mind fixed on the coming of the Messiah. His vivid dreams continued, and though he shared them with her, there was an urgency in his voice that concerned her.

One night, after another long day of work, Elijah awoke suddenly from one of his dreams. He sat up, his breath coming in quick, shallow gasps, his heart pounding in his chest. The vision had been so clear, so real—the child in Bethlehem, wrapped in cloths, lying in a humble dwelling, surrounded by light. A star shone overhead, and in the distance, the sounds of rejoicing filled the air.

"Elijah," Miriam whispered, stirring beside him. "What is it?"

Elijah turned to her, his eyes wide with a mixture of fear and awe. "The child," he said, his voice trembling. "He's coming. Soon."

Miriam reached for his hand, her fingers warm and steady. "It's just a dream," she said softly, though she knew that, for Elijah, it was more than that. "You need to rest."

But Elijah couldn't rest. The dream had shaken him to his core, and he felt as though the prophecy was unfolding before his very eyes. He rose from the bed, his hands shaking as he reached for the scroll of Micah, unrolling it carefully as he read the familiar words again and again.

"But you, Bethlehem Ephrathah... out of you will come for me one who will be ruler over Israel..."

The words burned in his mind, filling him with a sense of urgency that he couldn't ignore. The Messiah was coming. He had to be. Elijah had seen Him—felt His presence in the dreams—and now, more than ever, he believed that their work, their sacrifices, had all been leading to this moment.

As the weeks passed, Elijah's dreams became more frequent, and the strain on his body and mind grew more intense. Miriam, now in the later stages of her pregnancy, watched him with increasing concern. She could see the toll the visions were taking on him, but she also understood the depth of his faith. Elijah was not one to shy away from the weight of the prophecies, and now, with the dream of the Messiah so close, he was determined to be ready.

Abba Nathan, too, had noticed the change in Elijah. One afternoon, as they worked together on transcribing a particularly fragile scroll, the elder spoke quietly to him. "You are carrying much, Elijah. But remember, the prophecies unfold in their own time. We are part of that unfolding, but we cannot force it."

Elijah nodded, though his mind was elsewhere. He knew Abba Nathan was right, but the dreams felt too real, too urgent to ignore.

"Focus on the words," Nathan continued, his voice gentle but firm. "They will guide you. The Messiah will come when the time is right."

Elijah looked at the elder, his heart heavy with the weight of the dreams. "What if the time is now?" he asked, his voice barely above a whisper.

Abba Nathan smiled faintly, his eyes full of wisdom. "Then you will be ready. But remember, it is not just you who prepares the way. We all do."

As Miriam's time drew near, the entire community of Qumran gathered around her, supporting her as she prepared for the birth of their child. There was a sense of anticipation, not just for the new life that was about to be born, but for what it represented. This child, like Miriam herself, was a symbol of hope—a sign that life continued, even after the darkest of times.

Elijah, though exhausted, found himself more deeply connected to Miriam than ever before. He watched her, marveling at her strength and resilience. She had always been a guiding force for him, and now, as she prepared to give birth, he felt a renewed sense of purpose.

The night their child was born, the stars were bright above Qumran, the air filled with a quiet stillness. Elijah stayed close to Miriam's side, his heart pounding as he waited. The labor was long, but Miriam remained strong, her eyes filled with determination.

When the baby's first cry pierced the air, Elijah felt a surge of emotion so powerful that it left him breathless. He knelt beside Miriam, tears streaming down his face as he looked at their child—a tiny, perfect life, born into a world that had seen so much suffering, but was now filled with hope.

"It's a boy," one of the women said softly, handing the child to Miriam.

Miriam smiled, her face glowing with a mixture of exhaustion and joy. She looked at Elijah, her eyes bright with love and hope. "Our son," she whispered.

Elijah reached out, his hand trembling as he touched the child's tiny head. In that moment, all of his fears, all of his doubts, melted away. This child—this precious new life—was the future. He wasn't the Messiah, but he was part of the story, part of the unfolding plan that Elijah had dedicated his life to.

And as Elijah held his son for the first time, he felt a peace settle over him, a peace that came from knowing that, no matter what the future held, the work they had done, the sacrifices they had made, had been worth it.

The Messiah would come. In His time, in His way.

And Elijah would be ready.

The days after their son's birth were filled with a quiet joy that Elijah hadn't known in years. The weight of the prophecies, the strain of the journey, and the pain of loss had dulled the vibrancy of life for so long, but now, as he held his son, he felt the warmth of hope stirring within him once again. His son's tiny fingers wrapped around his, and in that touch, Elijah sensed a future full of possibilities.

Miriam, though physically weary from the labor, glowed with a peace that seemed to radiate outward, bringing comfort to all who were around her. She was the center of Qumran's small community now, the symbol of life's continuity. With each passing day, she and Elijah found themselves speaking in softer tones, as if not to disturb the fragile new hope their child embodied.

The boy had been named Nathaniel, in honor of Abba Nathan, whose wisdom had carried them through the darkest moments of their struggle. The elder had smiled when Elijah told him, a light shining in his tired eyes. "A fitting name for one who will carry the hope of his people," Abba Nathan had said, his voice full of gratitude.

As Elijah watched his son sleep one quiet afternoon, he felt that deep connection to the prophecies return, but this time, it wasn't accompanied by the same intensity that had once consumed him. He still believed the Messiah's coming was near, but holding Nathaniel in his arms, Elijah began to realize that the fulfillment of prophecy wasn't only about a distant, divine figure. It was about the choices they made now, the lives they nurtured, and the future they built. The Messiah's arrival was only one part of a larger story—one that included all of them.

The work at Qumran continued, though the pace had slowed since the baby's arrival. The scribes and scholars, still recovering from the physical and emotional toll of the revolt, had found new energy in the birth of Nathaniel. He was a living symbol of the next generation, of the future they were all fighting to protect. The community gathered frequently to check on Miriam and the child, offering small gifts and words of encouragement. In those moments, it was as if the entire weight of the past lifted, even if only for a few hours.

But for Elijah, life remained split between the joy of his family and the weight of the prophecies. His dreams had not stopped. Every few nights, he would awake, heart pounding, with visions of the child from Bethlehem lingering in his mind. He could see the star, shining brightly above the humble dwelling, and he could feel the weight of destiny on the child's shoulders. Elijah had come to believe that these dreams were not simply the product of an overburdened mind but divine messages. The arrival of the Messiah, the child prophesied in Micah 5:2, was imminent.

Miriam, however, had become more concerned as time went on. Elijah's obsession with the prophecies seemed to grow, even as his love for their son deepened. She understood his need to prepare, to be ready for the Messiah's arrival, but she also feared that Elijah was losing sight of the present, of the life they were building together. There was a distance between them, a growing sense that Elijah's focus was shifting entirely toward the unseen future.

One evening, as the sun set behind the desert hills, Miriam sat beside Elijah, their son sleeping peacefully between them. The orange glow of the setting sun cast long shadows over the rocky landscape, and for a moment, it felt as though time had slowed, giving them a brief reprieve from the pressures of the world.

"Elijah," Miriam said softly, her voice full of gentle concern, "you've been distant lately."

Elijah looked at her, surprised. "Distant?"

Miriam nodded, her eyes filled with quiet understanding. "You've been so focused on the dreams, on the prophecies. I know they're important—I know the Messiah is coming—but we have a life here, now. We have Nathaniel. I don't want you to miss these moments with him, with us."

Elijah felt a pang of guilt. He hadn't realized how deeply he'd been consumed by his visions. The prophecies had always been his guiding light, but now, with Nathaniel in his life, he was beginning to see that his role in the story wasn't just about preserving the Word for future generations. It was about living in the present, too—about being a father, a husband, a part of this community.

"I'm sorry, Miriam," he said quietly, his voice filled with sincerity. "I didn't mean to lose sight of what's right in front of me. The dreams... they've been so vivid, so real. It feels like the Messiah is closer than ever, and I've been trying to prepare."

Miriam reached out and took his hand, her touch gentle but firm. "I know. And we will prepare, together. But we also have to live, Elijah. We have to be here for Nathaniel, for each other. The future will come, but we can't lose ourselves in it."

Elijah looked at her, the weight of her words sinking in. He had spent so long focusing on what was to come that he had nearly forgotten the importance of what was already here. Miriam was right. They couldn't live entirely in the future. Their son, their family, needed him now.

"You're right," Elijah said, squeezing her hand. "I don't want to miss any of this. I don't want to miss our life together."

Miriam smiled softly, relief washing over her. "We'll be ready when the time comes, Elijah. But for now, let's be present, here and now."

Over the next few weeks, Elijah worked to balance his focus between the prophecies and his family. He spent more time with Nathaniel, marveling at how quickly the boy was growing. He would sit with Miriam in the evenings, watching the stars appear in the desert sky, and for the first time in what felt like years, Elijah allowed himself to be still. The dreams still came, but they no longer dominated his every thought. He had learned, with Miriam's help, to let them guide him without letting them consume him.

Abba Nathan, sensing Elijah's shift in focus, took the opportunity to deepen his conversations with him about the prophecies of Malachi. "The victory in Jerusalem was a sign," Nathan said one day as they worked together in the scriptorium. "The temple has been cleansed, just as Daniel foretold. But this is only the beginning. The messenger, the one who will prepare the way for the Messiah, is coming. Our work is far from over."

Elijah nodded, his heart steady now as he listened to Nathan's words. "The cleansing of the temple felt like a fulfillment, but I know there is more to come. I've seen it in my dreams, Nathan. The child in Bethlehem... He's coming soon."

Nathan smiled gently, his old eyes gleaming with wisdom. "I believe you, Elijah. The signs are all around us. But remember, the work we do here is just as important as the dreams. We are preparing the way, not just for ourselves, but for those who will come after us. The prophecies must be preserved, passed down to future generations."

Elijah glanced at the scrolls before him, feeling the weight of their mission settle over him once again. He understood now, more clearly than ever, that their work in Qumran was not just for the present but for the future. They were the keepers of the Word, and it was their duty to ensure that the prophecies lived on, long after they were gone.

"We will be ready," Elijah said quietly. "When the Messiah comes, the Word will be ready."

As the months passed, life in Qumran began to settle into a new rhythm. The community, still recovering from the raid, had slowly begun to rebuild. The scribes and scholars worked diligently to restore what had been lost, and though their numbers were smaller now, there was a renewed sense of purpose among them. The birth of Nathaniel had brought new life to the group, a reminder that the future was still full of hope.

Miriam, now fully recovered from the birth, took on a more active role in the community, helping to organize the work and care for those who were still healing. Her presence was a source of strength for the group, and she often spoke to them about the prophecies, reminding them that the victory in Jerusalem was just the beginning.

"The Messiah will come," she would say, her voice filled with quiet certainty. "And when He does, we will be ready."

Elijah, too, found himself more at peace than he had been in years. The dreams still came, and he still believed that the Messiah's arrival was imminent, but he had learned to live in the present as well. He spent his days working with the scrolls, preserving the words of the prophets, and his nights with Miriam and Nathaniel, finding joy in the simple moments of family life.

One night, as they sat together beneath the stars, Elijah looked over at Miriam, his heart full of gratitude. "You were right," he said softly. "I was so focused on the future that I almost missed what was right in front of me."

Miriam smiled, her eyes warm. "The future is important, Elijah. But so is the present. We're building something here, something that will last."

Elijah nodded, his gaze drifting to the sleeping form of their son. "Nathaniel will grow up in a different world, a world where the Word is preserved, where the prophecies live on."

"And the Messiah," Miriam added, her voice full of hope. "He will come, Elijah. I believe that with all my heart."

Elijah took her hand, his grip gentle but firm. "So do I," he said quietly. "And when He does, we will be ready."

Chapter 9: The Voice in the Wilderness

The sun sat low in the sky, casting long shadows over the barren hills of Qumran. Time had passed, though the weight of the years had been softened by the quiet peace that now filled Elijah's life. His hands, though worn with age, still moved skillfully over the scrolls as he copied the sacred words, preserving the texts with the same reverence he had carried for decades. His hair, once dark, was now streaked with gray, and his body, though still strong, felt the ache of age in the early morning hours. But Elijah was at peace.

Nathaniel, now a young man, had grown into a quiet, thoughtful soul, much like his father. He had spent years learning the ways of the scribes, his own hands now skilled in the art of transcribing the sacred texts. Miriam, too, had aged gracefully, her eyes still bright with the same hope and resilience that had carried them through their most difficult days. Their life, though simple, was full—anchored in the faith that had sustained them through every trial.

But something had begun to stir in the world beyond Qumran, a ripple in the spiritual fabric that had, for so long, felt silent. The rumors began as whispers—talk of a man preaching in the wilderness near the Jordan River. His name was John, and he spoke with the authority of a prophet. His message was simple yet profound: repentance, the coming of the kingdom of God, and the arrival of someone greater—someone whose sandals he was not worthy to untie.

Elijah first heard of John the Baptist through a traveler who passed through Qumran, seeking refuge for a night. The man's words were filled with awe as he spoke of the preacher's fiery sermons and the multitudes that flocked to hear him. But it was something deeper that stirred in Elijah's heart as the man recounted John's message of repentance and the coming kingdom.

"He's a voice in the wilderness," the traveler had said, his eyes wide with wonder. "Like a prophet of old, calling us back to God."

The words had struck something deep within Elijah. Malachi 3:1 came to his mind immediately: "Behold, I send my messenger, and he will prepare the way before me." The prophecy he had devoted his life to preserving was unfolding before his very eyes. A messenger, preparing the way for the Lord. Elijah's heart pounded in his chest as the traveler continued.

"He baptizes people in the Jordan River," the traveler added. "Says it's a sign of repentance, a washing away of sins before the coming of the Messiah."

The Messiah.

Elijah had known this day would come, though in his old age, he had begun to wonder if he would live to see it. The dreams he had once experienced so vividly had faded over the years, replaced by a quiet, steady faith that the prophecies would come to pass. But now, hearing of this John, Elijah knew—this was the moment he had been waiting for.

Days passed, and Elijah could think of little else but the man preaching in the wilderness. The words of the prophets, particularly Malachi, echoed in his mind, urging him to act, to go and see for himself. He had lived his life in service to the Word, preserving the scrolls, teaching his son, and supporting his community. But this—this was different. This was the fulfillment of everything he had worked for, everything he had believed.

One evening, as the stars began to dot the desert sky, Elijah sat with Miriam and Nathaniel outside their small home. The air was cool, and the soft hum of the wind over the hills provided a peaceful backdrop to their quiet conversation.

"I'm going to find him," Elijah said suddenly, breaking the comfortable silence.

Miriam looked at him, her expression calm but curious. "Find who?"

"John," Elijah replied, his voice steady with purpose. "The man they call the Baptist. I've heard enough to know he is the one spoken of in Malachi. He's the messenger, Miriam. He's preparing the way for the Messiah."

Nathaniel's eyes widened slightly, and Miriam's lips parted as if to respond, but she paused. She could see in Elijah's face that this wasn't just another moment of curiosity. There was a deep conviction in his words, a certainty that she had only seen a few times in their long life together. He truly believed this was the fulfillment of the prophecies.

"You believe this man is the one who will lead us to the Messiah?" Miriam asked softly, her voice filled with the same faith that had carried them both through so much.

Elijah nodded. "I do. And I need to see it for myself. I've spent my life preserving the words of the prophets, waiting for this day. I can feel it, Miriam. The time is near."

Miriam studied him for a long moment, then reached out and took his hand, her touch warm and steady. "Then go," she said gently. "Go and see."

Nathaniel, who had been listening quietly, leaned forward. "I'll go with you, Father."

Elijah smiled, a deep sense of gratitude swelling in his chest. His son—his beloved Nathaniel—was now a man, ready to walk beside him on this journey. He nodded, his voice filled with pride. "Yes, we'll go together."

The journey to the Jordan River was long, but Elijah and Nathaniel moved with purpose. As they traveled, Elijah felt a strange sense of calm wash over him. He had been waiting for this moment for so long, and now that it was here, he found himself at peace. The questions and doubts that had once plagued him had fallen away, replaced by a quiet certainty that everything was unfolding exactly as it was meant to.

When they finally arrived at the banks of the Jordan, the scene before them was unlike anything Elijah had ever seen. Crowds of people had gathered along the river, their faces filled with a mixture of awe and anticipation. In the center of it all stood a man—tall, wild-haired, with eyes that seemed to burn with an inner fire. He was waist-deep in the river, his hands raised as he spoke to the gathered crowd.

"Repent!" the man called, his voice carrying over the water. "Repent, for the kingdom of heaven is at hand!"

Elijah felt his breath catch in his throat. This was John. The voice in the wilderness. The one who had been sent to prepare the way.

Nathaniel, standing beside him, whispered in awe. "He speaks with such power."

Elijah nodded, his heart pounding in his chest. John's words were filled with authority, but they also carried the weight of prophecy. Every sentence seemed to echo with the fulfillment of Malachi's words, as if the very air around him was alive with the presence of something divine.

They stood at the edge of the crowd, listening as John spoke of repentance, of turning back to God, of preparing for the one who was to come. Elijah's mind raced as he took in every word, feeling the connection between the prophecies he had spent his life preserving and the message that was now being preached before him.

As the sermon came to an end, people began to move toward the river, seeking to be baptized. Elijah hesitated for a moment, then turned to Nathaniel.

"I need to speak with him," Elijah said quietly.

Nathaniel nodded. "I'll wait here."

Elijah made his way through the crowd, his heart racing as he approached the water's edge. John stood at the center of the river, his gaze fixed on the horizon, as if he were looking for something—or someone.

"John," Elijah called, his voice steady but filled with urgency.

The Baptist turned, his wild eyes locking onto Elijah's with a piercing intensity. For a moment, neither of them spoke, and Elijah felt as though the weight of heaven itself had settled between them.

"I've come to see the one who prepares the way," Elijah said, his voice barely a whisper. "I believe you are the messenger."

John studied him for a moment, then nodded slowly, as if he had expected Elijah's arrival. "I am the voice," John replied, his voice low and filled with purpose. "The one crying out in the wilderness, as Isaiah said. But I am not the one you seek."

Elijah's heart skipped a beat. "Then who?"

John's eyes burned with a fierce certainty as he spoke. "There is another. One greater than I. I baptize with water, but He will baptize with the Holy Spirit and with fire. He is already among us."

Elijah felt a chill run down his spine. "Who is He?"

John's gaze softened, his voice almost reverent as he answered. "Jesus of Nazareth. He is the Lamb of God, who takes away the sins of the world."

The name struck Elijah like a thunderclap. Jesus of Nazareth. The Messiah. The one he had waited his entire life for. He had dreamed of Him, seen glimpses of His coming in the words of the prophets, and now, He was here.

Elijah's knees weakened, and for a moment, he felt as though the weight of everything—the years of waiting, the years of preserving the prophecies—was pressing down on him all at once.

"The Messiah..." Elijah whispered, his voice filled with awe.

John nodded, his face calm and full of a quiet certainty. "Yes. He is here."

That night, Elijah and Nathaniel camped by the river, the stars shining brightly overhead. Elijah lay awake, his mind filled with the words of John the Baptist. Jesus of Nazareth. The Lamb of God. It was all coming together—the prophecies, the dreams, the years of waiting. The Messiah had come, and the world was about to change forever.

Nathaniel, sensing the weight of the moment, sat beside his father in silence for a long while before speaking.

"Do you believe this is really Him?" Nathaniel asked softly, his voice filled with wonder.

Elijah nodded, his heart full. "I do. This is what we've been waiting for, Nathaniel. Everything we've done—preserving the scrolls, living through the revolt, all the suffering—it's all been leading to this. The Messiah has come."

Nathaniel's eyes shone with the same hope that had once filled Elijah in his younger days. "And now?"

Elijah smiled, a deep peace settling over him. "Now, we continue to prepare the way. John was right—our work is not finished. We may have preserved the prophecies, but there are still many who have not yet heard. We will carry the message forward, just as John is doing."

Nathaniel nodded, his heart swelling with purpose. "We'll make sure the world knows."

The years that followed were marked by a quiet, reflective faith in Elijah's life. He and Nathaniel returned to Qumran, but the fire of the coming kingdom burned in their hearts. News of Jesus of Nazareth spread, and though Elijah never met Him face to face, he knew, deep in his soul, that the Messiah's work had begun. The prophecies were being fulfilled, and Elijah, now nearing the end of his life, felt a profound peace settle over him.

Miriam, too, shared in this peace. As they sat together in the twilight of their years, watching their son carry on the work they had started, they both knew that their part in the story was complete. They had preserved the Word, prepared the way, and now, the kingdom was unfolding before their very eyes.

And as Elijah watched the sun set over the desert one last time, he smiled, knowing that the voice in the wilderness had spoken the truth. The Messiah had come. And the world would never be the same.

The sun sat high in the sky as Elijah and Nathaniel moved with the crowd, their footsteps blending into the throng of people who had gathered in the countryside. The air buzzed with excitement and anticipation. Word had spread quickly through the villages and towns that Jesus of Nazareth was nearby, and thousands had come to see Him, hear His teachings, and witness the miracles that were said to follow wherever He went.

Elijah's heart raced as they walked, surrounded by men, women, and children—people from every corner of Judea and Galilee. The journey to find Jesus had not been an easy one, but Elijah and Nathaniel had been sustained by their faith, driven by the certainty that they were about to witness something extraordinary. Yet even now, as the crowds swelled and the dust of their sandals filled the air, Elijah knew that his desire to meet the Messiah face-to-face might not be fulfilled today. There were simply too many people.

But Elijah had long since accepted that the ways of God were often mysterious, unfolding in ways that humans could not predict. The Messiah's presence was enough. He was here, in the midst of His people, and Elijah's heart was content to know that he was close, even if he didn't stand before Him personally.

The crowd pressed in around them as they reached the grassy hillside. People were settling down, finding places to sit and wait, their voices low with murmurs of anticipation. Elijah glanced at Nathaniel, who was watching the crowd with wide eyes.

"Look how many have come," Nathaniel whispered, awe filling his voice. "They've all come to see Him."

Elijah smiled, feeling the same wonder. "Yes," he said softly. "The world is waking up."

As they moved further into the crowd, the sea of people seemed endless. The sight of so many gathered to hear Jesus reminded Elijah of the prophecies he had cherished for so long. Isaiah had spoken of the day when the nations would be drawn to the light of God's chosen one, and Elijah knew in his heart that this was the beginning of that fulfillment.

They found a place to sit on the hillside, close enough to see the figures moving in the distance. Though they could not see Jesus clearly, Elijah could hear His voice, calm and steady, as He taught the people. His words carried across the crowd like a breeze, filling the air with a peace that Elijah had not felt since his dreams of the child in Bethlehem.

For hours, they sat, listening, soaking in the teachings. Elijah closed his eyes at times, letting the words wash over him, each one confirming what he already knew deep in his soul. This was the Messiah. The one who had been foretold. Every sentence, every parable, felt like the culmination of the prophecies he had spent his life preserving.

But as the day wore on, Elijah began to notice the restlessness in the crowd. People were growing hungry, and children tugged at their mothers' clothes, asking when they would eat. Elijah himself felt the familiar pangs of hunger but pushed them aside, content to remain where he was.

Nathaniel, however, was watching the crowd closely. "Father," he said quietly, "the people are hungry. They've come from far away. What will they do?"

Elijah looked around, seeing the concern on the faces of those nearby. The crowd was enormous—thousands of people—and there was no food in sight, no way to feed so many. Elijah felt a brief flicker of worry but reminded himself that they were in the presence of the Messiah. If anyone could provide for them, it was Him.

As if in answer to his thoughts, Elijah saw movement near the front of the crowd. One of Jesus' disciples—a man Elijah recognized as Philip—was speaking with Jesus, gesturing toward the crowd. Though Elijah couldn't hear their words, he could see the concern on Philip's face as he spoke.

Nathaniel leaned in closer, trying to catch what was happening. "What's going on?"

"I don't know," Elijah said, his eyes fixed on the scene ahead. "But watch. Something is about to happen."

Moments later, another disciple—Andrew—stepped forward, holding a small basket in his hands. Elijah squinted, trying to see what was inside. A few loaves of bread, perhaps, and some fish. Hardly enough to feed a family, let alone the thousands that were gathered here.

The crowd murmured, noticing the exchange, but Elijah remained silent, his heart steady. He had seen miracles before in his life. He had witnessed God's provision in ways that defied explanation. But this—this felt different. There was something in the air, a stillness, a sense that they were on the verge of witnessing something extraordinary.

Then, Jesus lifted His hands.

The crowd grew silent as Jesus blessed the small offering of bread and fish. His voice, though soft, carried across the hillside, and Elijah felt a shiver run down his spine as the words of Psalm 23 echoed in his mind: "The Lord is my shepherd; I shall not want. He makes me lie down in green pastures."

Without warning, the disciples began moving through the crowd, distributing the bread and fish. Elijah watched in awe as the baskets seemed to multiply, as if the food was being created out of thin air. Nathaniel gasped beside him, his eyes wide with disbelief.

"Father... look!"

Elijah nodded, too overcome to speak. He watched as the food was passed from person to person, each one receiving enough to satisfy their hunger. What had started as a few loaves and fish was now feeding thousands. Elijah could hardly believe what he was seeing, but he knew, without a doubt, that this was a sign. The Messiah was not only a spiritual redeemer—He was a provider, a shepherd to His people, caring for their physical needs as well as their souls.

As the disciples drew nearer, one of them handed Elijah and Nathaniel bread and fish. Elijah accepted it with trembling hands, bowing his head in silent gratitude. He glanced at Nathaniel, who was staring at the food in his hands, his expression one of pure awe.

"This is a miracle," Nathaniel whispered.

Elijah nodded, his heart full. "Yes," he said softly. "It is."

They ate in silence, the bread and fish filling their stomachs, but it was more than just food. It was a reminder—a confirmation—that they were witnessing the work of the Messiah. Elijah's mind raced with the words of the prophets, especially Isaiah 55:1: "Come, all you who are thirsty, come to the waters; and you who have no money, come, buy and eat!"

This was what they had been waiting for. The kingdom of God was not just a promise for the future—it was unfolding before their very eyes.

As the sun began to set, the crowd slowly dispersed, their hearts and stomachs full from the day's events. Elijah and Nathaniel remained seated for a while longer, the warmth of the evening settling over them like a blanket. Elijah's thoughts drifted back to his life, to the years he had spent waiting, preparing, preserving the Word. And now, here he was, witnessing the fulfillment of those prophecies in ways he had never imagined.

"I didn't expect this," Nathaniel said quietly, breaking the silence.

Elijah smiled, understanding what his son meant. "Neither did I. But that's how God works. His ways are higher than ours."

Nathaniel nodded, his face thoughtful. "I thought we might meet Him. I thought we might stand before Him and hear His voice."

Elijah looked at his son, his heart full of love and pride. "We didn't need to stand before Him, Nathaniel. We've seen His work. We've felt His presence. That is enough."

Nathaniel was silent for a moment, then smiled softly. "You're right, Father. It is enough."

Elijah leaned back, gazing up at the stars as they began to appear in the sky. The Messiah had come, and though Elijah had not stood face-to-face with Him, he had seen the evidence of His kingdom in the miracle they had just witnessed. His heart was full, his soul at peace.

The prophecies had been fulfilled. The Word had been preserved. And now, Elijah's work was complete.

Epilogue: The Eternal Word

Qumran, 30 CE

The sun dipped low behind the jagged cliffs of the Judean desert, casting the last of its light over the ancient caves of Qumran. The familiar wind, which had swept across this barren landscape for centuries, whispered through the narrow passages, rustling the leaves of the palm trees that clung to life near the shores of the Dead Sea. But this time, the wind carried more than just the desert sands; it carried the echoes of a legacy, a story that spanned generations.

Elijah had passed away quietly in his sleep, his aged body finally succumbing to the years of faithful labor he had carried out with quiet dignity. He had been an old man, his face weathered with time and experience, but his heart had remained as steadfast as ever. His passing, though marked by sorrow, had also brought a sense of peace to the community. Those who had known him, including his son Nathaniel and his beloved Miriam, knew that his life's mission had been fulfilled.

In the years that followed Elijah's death, Qumran continued to serve as a sanctuary for the preservation of the sacred texts. The scribes, many of whom had been trained by Elijah and Nathaniel, worked tirelessly, copying scroll after scroll, ensuring that the words of the prophets would survive the ravages of time. Though the world around them was changing—Rome's power spreading and wars brewing—the quiet, persistent work of the scribes remained the same.

But the true legacy Elijah had left behind wasn't just in the ink and parchment. It was in the hearts of those who had worked beside him, in the lives of those who had listened to his teachings, and in the faith that had been passed down from generation to generation. His life had been a thread in the tapestry of God's divine plan, and though he was now gone, that thread remained strong, woven into the fabric of history.

A Future Unseen

Centuries passed, and Qumran, like many other places, felt the shifting tides of empires. The Roman legions marched across Judea, and the world that Elijah had known began to change. But in the remote caves of Qumran, something more enduring than any empire was being preserved—the Word of God, the prophecies, the history of a people waiting for their Messiah.

The scribes had hidden the scrolls away, carefully placing them in clay jars, sealing them from the elements, and storing them in the cool, dry caves that overlooked the Dead Sea. They knew that the world outside was unpredictable, but here, in these quiet caves, the sacred texts would remain, untouched by time, until the world was ready for them again.

Nathaniel had taken up his father's mantle after Elijah's death. His hands, much like his father's, had grown skilled at transcribing the texts, and his heart had been filled with the same reverence for the Word. As he grew older, Nathaniel became known among the scribes as a faithful guardian, just as Elijah had been. He had carried his father's legacy forward, teaching the next generation the importance of preserving the Word, of waiting for the promises of God to be fulfilled.

And yet, as the years turned into decades and the decades into centuries, Qumran became a memory. The community that had once flourished slowly faded, its people scattered, and the caves, once bustling with activity, grew silent.

Jerusalem, 70 CE

In the years after Jesus' crucifixion and resurrection, Jerusalem fell into turmoil. The temple, once the center of Jewish life, was destroyed by Roman forces, and the people scattered. The world that Elijah had once lived in had changed beyond recognition. The prophets had spoken of such days, of destruction and scattering, of the trials that would come before the final redemption.

But even in this time of chaos, there were those who still clung to the words of the prophets, to the hope of a new kingdom, a kingdom not of this world. The early Christian believers, many of whom had followed Jesus during His ministry, began to spread His message across the Roman Empire. They spoke of Him as the fulfillment of the prophecies, the Lamb of God who had taken away the sins of the world.

The prophecies that Elijah and the scribes had spent their lives preserving were now being fulfilled in the most unexpected ways. Jesus of Nazareth, the man Elijah had heard of in his later years, had indeed been the Messiah, just as John the Baptist had foretold. His life, death, and resurrection had become the cornerstone of a new faith, a faith that would spread across the world, carrying with it the fulfillment of the ancient prophecies.

Centuries Later: The Discovery

It was 1947, centuries after Qumran had fallen silent, when a young Bedouin shepherd stumbled upon a cave in the cliffs near the Dead Sea. He had been searching for a lost goat when he threw a stone into the cave, hoping to startle the animal. Instead of hearing the soft bleating of a goat, the shepherd heard the distinct sound of pottery shattering.

Curious, the young man climbed into the cave, his heart racing as he made his way through the narrow passage. What he found would change the course of biblical history. There, hidden in clay jars, were ancient scrolls—scrolls that had been preserved for nearly two thousand years.

The discovery of the Dead Sea Scrolls was nothing short of miraculous. As archaeologists and scholars began to examine the fragile texts, they realized that they had uncovered one of the most important collections of ancient manuscripts in history. These scrolls included fragments of nearly every book of the Hebrew Bible, as well as other writings from the time of the Second Temple period.

Among the scrolls were the very prophecies that Elijah had spent his life preserving. Isaiah, Micah, Malachi—the words that had foretold the coming of the Messiah, the words that had been hidden away for centuries, were now revealed to the world. The scrolls contained the prophecies of the suffering servant, of the voice in the wilderness, of the One who would be born in Bethlehem.

Elijah's legacy had not been lost. It had been preserved, waiting for the moment when the world would be ready to rediscover it.

As scholars studied the scrolls, they were struck by the way the ancient texts bridged the gap between the Old and New Testaments. The prophecies of the Old Testament, which had been fulfilled in the life of Jesus, were now laid bare, their words unchanged by the passage of time. It was as if the scrolls themselves testified to the truth of the Gospel, confirming that God's plan had been in motion all along.

A Legacy Beyond Time

Elijah's story had come full circle. The young scribe who had once watched his family die for their faith had become a faithful guardian of the Word, dedicating his life to preserving the prophecies that foretold the coming of the Messiah. Though he had not lived to see the full extent of the fulfillment, his life's work had played a crucial role in ensuring that the truth of the prophecies would endure.

Miriam's quiet strength and hope had sustained Elijah through the years, and though she too had passed, her influence remained. She had seen their son, Nathaniel, grow into a faithful man, carrying on the work that they had begun. And now, centuries later, the scrolls that they had labored over, that they had hidden away in the caves of Qumran, had been uncovered, their message intact.

The discovery of the Dead Sea Scrolls was more than just an archaeological marvel. It was a testament to the enduring nature of the Word of God. Elijah's life had been a single thread in the vast tapestry of God's plan, but that thread, woven together with the lives of so many others, had created a legacy that would outlast time itself.

In the words of the prophet Isaiah, which had been among the scrolls found in the caves, "The grass withers, the flower fades, but the word of our God will stand forever." (Isaiah 40:8)

Elijah's story had not ended with his death. It had continued, carried forward by the words he had so carefully preserved. And now, as the world rediscovered those words, his legacy lived on, a reminder that God's plan, no matter how long it takes, is always fulfilled.

The Final Fulfillment

As the scrolls were studied, the prophecies of the Old Testament were read anew. The prophecy of Isaiah 53, which spoke of a suffering servant who would bear the sins of many, resonated with those who knew the story of Jesus. The prophecy of Micah 5:2, which foretold that the ruler of Israel would come from Bethlehem, took on new meaning in light of Jesus' birth in that very town.

The link between the Old and New Testaments was undeniable. The scrolls confirmed what Elijah had spent his life believing—that the Messiah would come, and that His coming would change everything.

And so, Elijah's story, though rooted in the past, reached into the future, connecting the ancient prophecies to the fulfillment of God's plan in Jesus Christ. His life had been a journey of faith, of perseverance, of waiting for the promises of God. And in the end, those promises had been fulfilled, not just for Elijah, but for the world.

The scrolls, once hidden away in the desert caves of Qumran, had been revealed. And through them, the voice of Elijah, the voice of the prophets, continued to speak, reminding the world of the divine plan that had been written long ago, a plan that was still unfolding, even now.